SPORTING GUIDE

LOS ANGELES, 1897

LIZ GOLDWYN

Regan Arts.

For my father

CONTENTS

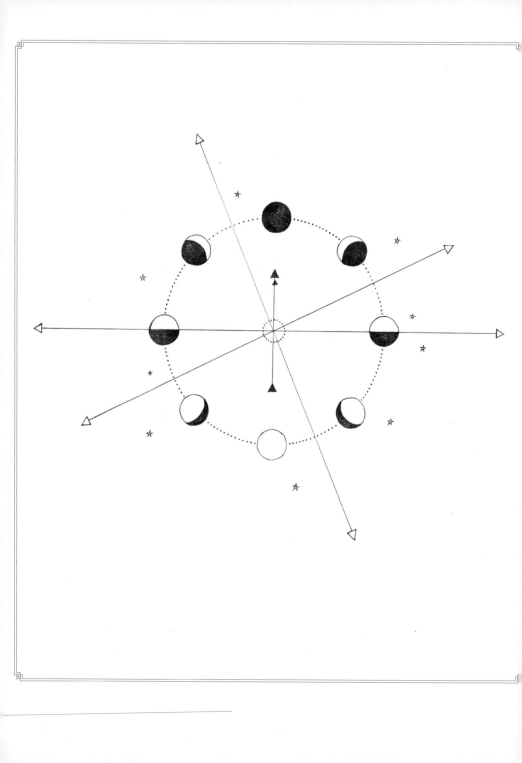

FOREWORD

There are moments when the boundaries between dimensions blur. Time is elastic, and you can slip right through, finding the ground you stand upon dissolving, coming back into focus centuries ago. And nothing and everything has changed. We are born, we die, we weep, and we love, just as we've always done.

This is the story of my time travel, to Los Angeles on the brink of the Industrial Age, and its power players—madams, crib lords, politicians, businessmen, and the forgotten women who served them.

Some of the characters in my tale once walked the same streets we do; others have been fictionalized. Many I have known and loved. Names have been changed to protect the identities of those still living, but the research and observations stem from fact. These are the stories of my hometown and the inhabitants I came to know through dusty archives, in hallucinations and dreams.

—Los Angeles, 2015

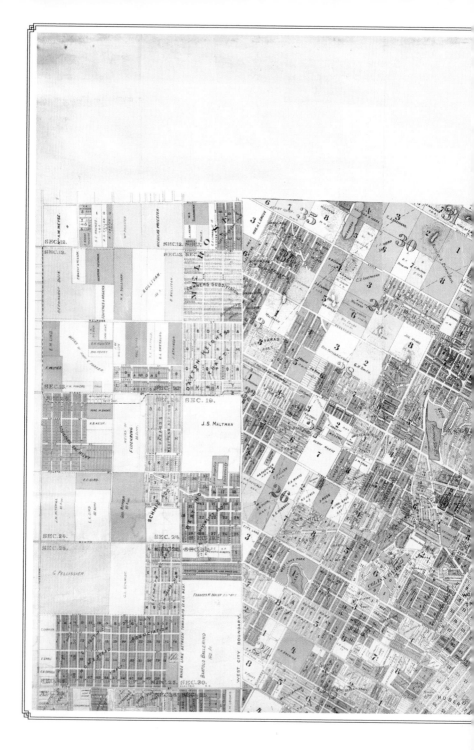

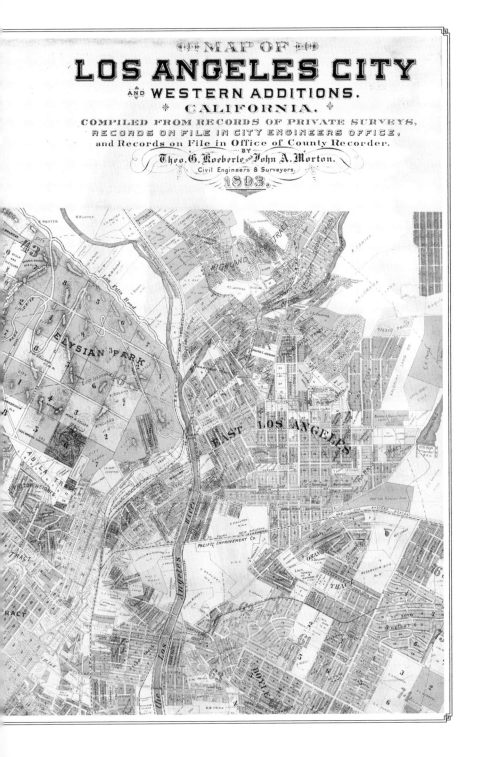

MAP OF
LOS ANGELES CITY
AND WESTERN ADDITIONS.
CALIFORNIA.

COMPILED FROM RECORDS OF PRIVATE SURVEYS,
RECORDS ON FILE IN CITY ENGINEERS OFFICE,
and Records on File in Office of County Recorder.

BY

Theo. G. Koeberle and John A. Morton.

Civil Engineers & Surveyors.

1893.

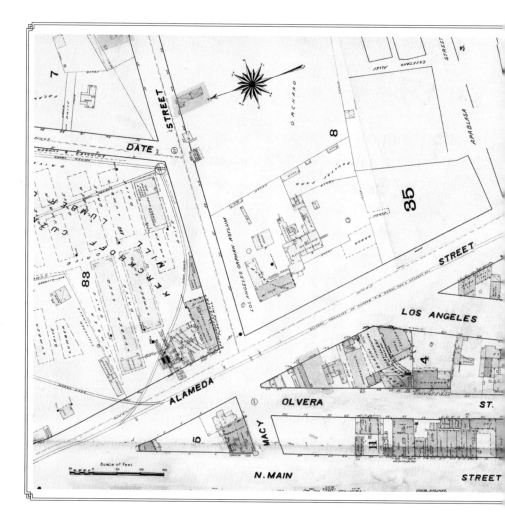

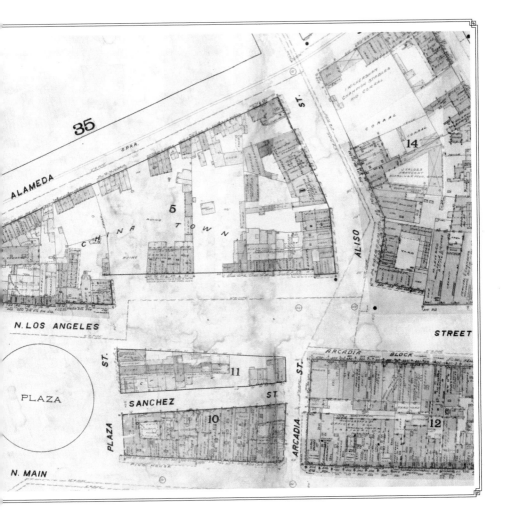

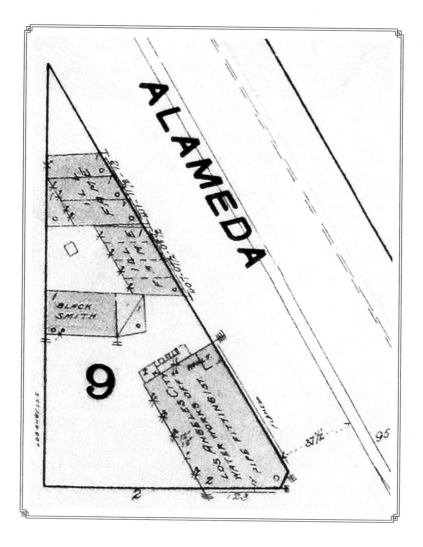

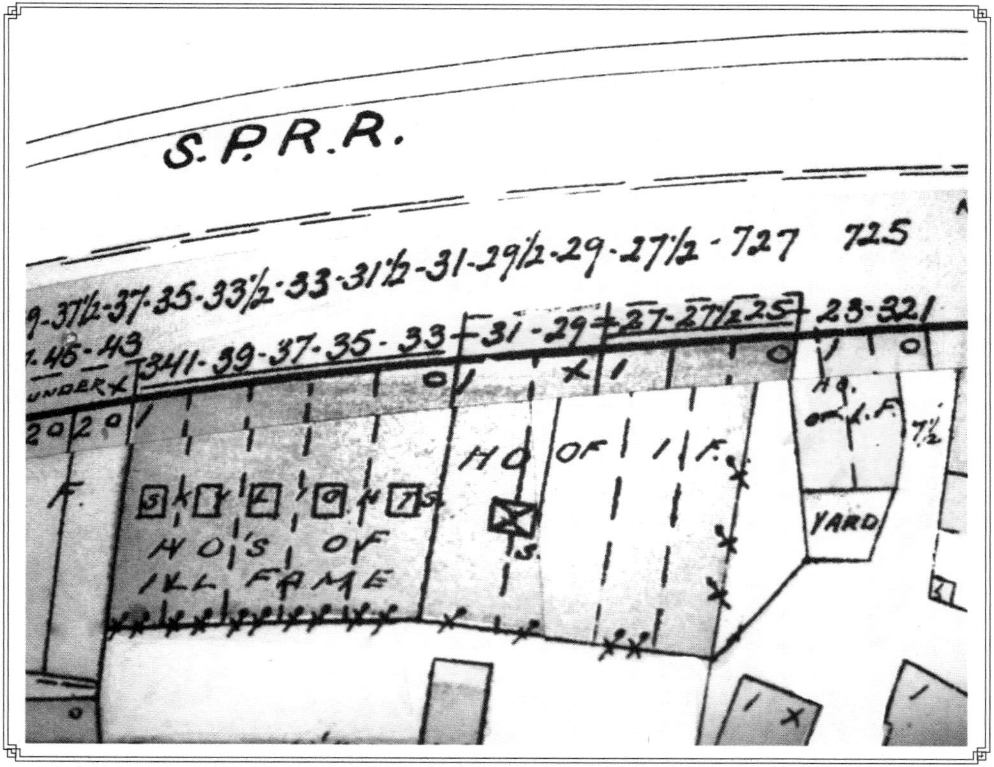
S.P.R.R.
725
HO'S OF
ILL FAME
HO OF I.F.
YARD

COURTHOUSE
BUILT IN
1859

CHAPTER ONE

A RIVALRY

If Los Angeles was a monarchy, I'd be its queen.

My castle, a formidable brick building to befit my position, sits on Marchessault Street. Inside, a full staff maneuvers among the finest furnishings gold can buy. Hell, I got two Steinway pianos and a crystal chandelier all the way from Vienna in my main parlor alone. The building used to be the county courthouse. Times have changed since I moved my operation here in 1891. And time is changing even faster now.

I've held my throne for more than two decades—ever since I settled in this city. Was the winter of 1877, around the time they renamed Nigger Alley to Los Angeles Street. Only place the name stuck is on the fire insurance maps—no one bothers much with formalities round here.

"Nigger Alley"
1882

I house sixteen ladies under my roof. Suppose you could say they're my crown jewels. See, I trade in premium pussy. Not like the dollar tricks you can find down in the Alley, in cheap crib-girl joints. I got bills to pay. You want my cunny, it'll cost you top dollar. Them reformers think we're all the same in my trade, but how much you pay for flesh depends on the class of service provided. We got a real defined pecking order. Sometimes I think about taking an advert in the new telephone directory just to turn off the penny-pinchers from knocking on my door trying to find a deal.

```
CASTLES........................NICEST    BROTHELS    $$$$

HOUSES...............RUN  BY  MID  LEVEL  MADAM  $$$

CRIBS.................CHEAP  GIRLS  /  DOLLAR  A  ROOM  $

DIVES............................................LOWEST  JOINTS  ¢
```

From Pasadena to the Port of Los Angeles, my palace of the purple arts is known as the finest. No one's got my menu of amusements, I'd like to see them just try.

I got a peephole room for rent overlooking a bedroom upstairs— plenty of my customers like to be observed while they perform. And dozens more pay an hourly rate for the view. For my lady customers—oh yes, I got a few of those too—I keep a separate afternoon schedule.

On Thursday evenings I present "poses plastiques" in the French style. When the clock strikes midnight, my houseman, Billy, announces the "show"—a living painting featuring six of my girls au natural re-creating one of them French masterpieces. Sometimes I get a girl from Chinatown if the customers want a slave-girl scene. Those China girls are being imported faster than any of the dry goods on Spring Street. Some came with the railroad workers, but that dirty crib lord Bartolo Ballerino got a brisk trade in girls sent down from 'Frisco to fill his hovels. Advertising them as "celestial females," known to carry all the mysterious secrets of the Orient. Hell, it ain't no secret how to screw.

They don't have proper American names, so we call 'em as the police book 'em:

"Pox-U"
"Me-Fuck"

But I usually stick to nice white girls. You can get those other types of freak shows elsewhere, thank you very much.

Madam Rosy over on Aliso Street has those "circus" acts going— one big orgy scene. I hear she's got a horse in one of those acts— too much to clean up after, if you ask me. I run a classy house, not some barnyard. If you've a taste for darkies, you can find them too at Madame Bolanger's The Octoroon at 438 North Alameda Street, but she lists them as "Oriental" on her booking records.

circa 1885

CHINESE SLAVE WOMEN CROSSING ALAMEDA STREET

If you ain't got much in your pocket, you can get a grown gray for very little. Those girls make themselves up to look like maidens with pigtails, bows, and painted angel lips, but I'll be damned if they ain't north of forty with their weary bodies and sagging jowls. And dollymops are plenty among the city's milliners, nursemaids, and dance-hall girls—they'll screw for the price of a beer. I charge a john fifty dollars just for the champagne while he watches one of my shows, on top of whatever private performance he wants to purchase after.

My customers are the ruling class of this city. Hell, Mayor "Pinky" Snyder holds nightly council meetings here—unofficially, of course—and the police department's on my payroll. Like I said, I got bills to pay. It ain't cheap to get the girls fixed up every month, plus laundry service, butlers, and valets— on top of paying graft to half the hacks and messenger boys in Los Angeles. Even my kitchen is known for its high-quality oysters and Pomona farm-fed

A familar figure around the market and Los Angeles streets about 1900. His coat was made of papers sewed together.

turkey roasts. After all, no man lives on bread alone. Got a list of accounts at the Central Market about a mile long. It tires me just to think about it.

I work hard maintaining the excellence of my castle. Goddam-nit! I've earned my bragging rights fair and square as the best madam in town. I even have my own box at the opera, with a gold placard bearing my name:

THE QUEEN'S BOX

PEARL MORTON

Guess you could say I was born into the sporting life. I didn't have a solid-gold spoon to teethe on—hell, no. My birthplace was a hog ranch, the lowest dive you could imagine. A real loathsome brothel situated right between a slaughterhouse and a saloon, just outside a military outpost in Jacksonville. The first sounds I ever heard were the screams of a pig squealing. I laugh now, but it wasn't no farm life, milking cows and picking daisies while Mother churned butter for hot biscuits.

By the time I was born, she was at the end of the line, an aged whore used up by the frontier. Dad was a john. I'd lay awake listening to her entertain, imagining each one of them was him. I never knew. I don't think she did, either. I shudder now thinking about the smell of that barn attic: wet manure, stale hay, and beer mixing with the sweat of the men.

I became a woman around eleven years old, before I was even bleeding. Mother asked what good a daughter was if she couldn't earn her keep? And that was that. Wasn't no room for discussion.

Mother's customers 'd give us small brass checks—coin tokens— in exchange for our services. Each house had its own imprint.

1 SILVER DOLLAR = 1 TOKEN

5 SILVER DOLLARS = 6 TOKENS

They'd put those tokens in our stockings before we got to screwing. Gotta make sure you get the money up front. Learned that fast. I didn't have fancy stockings in those days—no ribbons with tassels to tie them with. Mother used to wrap a piece of rough rope around the tops with frayed knots to keep 'em tight.

I hated that ranch. Hated the hogs and the soldiers with their cheap tips and Injin stories. I got out as soon as I was thirteen, when I met Annie, a working girl coming through from Canada on her way to New Orleans. She knew a Madame Laval that'd pay extra for a tenderfoot like me. I didn't need to hear that twice. I was out before I was gone. Might as well be making that coin for

Bawdy house coin for
Madame Bolanger's
The Octoroon

myself 'stead of giving it to Mother. Never looked back on that woman, those times—I spat on its grave and clean walked away.

I worked dive to joint to house, one small town after another. Hell, I stayed in eight different states before I was even twenty. Could hardly tell one cramped quarter from the next. I got a real good education those early years. I probably know men better than they know themselves—what they like, what their secrets are, and how much they'll spend to hush you up.

I kept a small black account ledger tucked under my mattress, keeping track of their peculiarities:

From Out of Town

A 31 year old retired millionaire with a fortune from
electric streetlights. Married at 20, 3 children, unhappy with
his wife. Friends travel to Europe to tour the finest brothels —
Venice, Paris, Rome. Claims not to partake; just likes to hear them
described. Pays someone to listen to him while he masturbates.
As frigid as the wife he loathes.

The Narcissist

Wants to be served and disciplined; someone to cook and
clean with a whip. High tolerance for pain; convinced he
cannot be hurt.

The Impotent Client

The Businessman

Keeps own records and receipts outside official books
and an expense account to cover visiting clients. Wife
tolerates his affairs; keeps her in the latest fashions
from Godey's Lady's Books, food on the table, gave her
children to look after. Really, a woman couldn't ask
for a better husband, if you asked him.

The Artist

Says it makes his life simpler to visit whores.
Doesn't want any distractions, complicated emotions.
Fears intimacy. Preoccupied with finding his "muse",
an endless series of lovers he tires of once they start
"needing me". Likes to see himself reflected in their
eyes. His art is his only true love.

The College Boy

In the morning he ate 3 bananas in a row as though
replacing his vitamin supply. Left his glasses under the bed.

The Virgin

His mother opened a house account so he wouldn't fall
in love with the first girl he bedded. She feared he'd
squander his inheritance on a bastard child. He fell
in love with a lady of the house instead. Comes four
times weekly to visit, charged direct to mother.

"*Actresses*" CROSSING the RIVER to a MINER'S CAMP

By the summer of '76 I was working out of Dolly Ogden's in San Francisco. Real nice parlor house with red velvet curtains and a gilt staircase she'd imported from Paris. I was almost grown gray by then, and I didn't have much trade, but Dolly liked me, and I had a regular—a widower—who came three nights a week. He was an accountant with ambitions of being a politician. Always respected ambition. I helped him get into office by blackmailing the local city council. Told you I knew secrets.

LAND LOTS FOR SALE

I took my earnings from that accountant and found a sizable tract of land right here in Los Angeles ten years before the real estate boom of '87. Of course I was a success straight away—had enough training by then. I brought in the highest rates in town for the snatch I sold. My black ledger had customers from Chicago to Texas—sporting men came from all over to see Madam Pearl. As my adopted city's railroad and citrus industries grew, so did my business—with all those newcomers who came to the land of sunshine and eternal youth. It meant more money for me.

CITY hALL AND JAIL

Spring & Franklin streets

Before long I was part of the tapestry of this city, accepted but not acknowledged in public by the ladies whose husbands were frequent visitors to my house. But their children still curtsy to me when they pass in the streets. I cut a fine figure in my afternoon dress of plum voile with satin stripes, black ostrich–plumed hat resting on top of my curls. Little girls can't help but be drawn to my colorful finery. And who can blame them?

My reputation rose alongside the capitalists setting up shop along Main Street downtown. You couldn't find a finer place in 'Frisco any day. I used to have brass coins placed in my stockings; now I keep a bankroll of notes. I've diamond rings on each finger and my table's set with plates of bacon.

Back at the hog farm I used to dream of being as rich as I am now. How happy I would be. But now, the more money I make, the more my problems grow.

I tell you, business ain't what it used to be. Longtime clients are dying off right and left—most of them had twenty years on me when I started in this town. Now the marketplace is crowded, and there's a whole new generation with too many choices. It gives me stomach pains just thinking about it. Got empty bottles of Burdock Blood Bitters clinking in my purse alongside my gold.

Didn't use to be I had much competition.

Madame Bolanger's a pest at most, and I don't give two farts

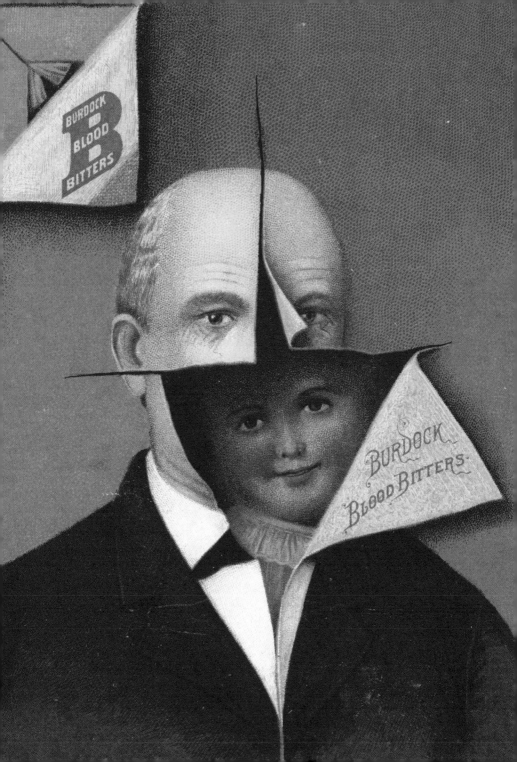

about that woman Stella Mitchell, Viola's Place is no better than housing for dollymops—collecting pocket change from easy pickings. If anyone forgets their place—and no one ever does—a well-placed bribe or a police raid does the job. They know I got the drop on them.

But Cora Phillips. That girl's another story altogether.

Appeared out of nowhere about ten months ago, that one. And I tell you no one sets up shop in this town without paying proper respect to the queen. So she starts out charging my prices to my clients . . . who does she think she is? Settling in on Alameda Street in that brick mansion with its stone lions guarding the place. People say her house—that damn house with its turrets and twining ivy—is the finest they've ever seen. Her girls the most elegant. Her pussy the sweetest. What's she got that I ain't got? They call her the "twenty-four-karat queen of Bohemia"—harrumph—like her twat's so precious. They all smell the same.

I don't like other people stepping on my toes. And I especially don't like being reminded of it. These days I can't go anywhere without someone speaking that damn woman's name. Gets to be so that people think I'm having trouble, start taking liberties with courtesy. Why, just yesterday afternoon down at the Basket Saloon I was meeting with Mayor Snyder and the Fat Man—he's my banker, and he keeps the payrolls for all the sporting houses of any note in this town, right alongside the genteel folk his bank serves—about a piece of business when who should go mixing in my affairs but that immigrant Ballerino?

The meeting was set for four o'clock, but when I got there, the three of them were already nursing half-smoked cigars and their second glasses of whiskey. Damned if the whole lot of them just sat there when I arrived. There's real trouble when they stop showing the proper respect to me. At least the Fat Man knew enough to pour me a glass.

We got to discussing a piece of land behind Nigger Alley that's coming up for sale. Pinky and Ballerino wanted to purchase it with city funds, but don't want their names on the title. We agreed on a fair trade to have me sign the deed and were just finishing up when Ballerino let slip a little insult on his way out the door.

"Nice doin' business with you, Pearly. Heard you was having a little trouble these days, that Cora Phillips be taking some of your best customers."

I started to respond, but the door was already swinging with his exit. The Fat Man was quick to assuage my anger.

"Don't mind him, Pearl. You know these Italian immigrant types—no manners at all. Cora may have a different class of broads, but she don't got your style."

I smiled at him graciously.

SPRING STREET, NORTH OF FIRST STREET, 1895

"Cora Phillips's girls ain't no different from his cheap twats—they're just trussed-up strumpets is all."

The Fat Man nodded in agreement. "Odd woman, that Phillips. She appeared out of nowhere. And that parlor house of hers was bought all in coin. Most sporting ladies come to see me after bank hours for a loan."

Pinky interrupted with a taunt. "And I bet you offer a fine rate of exchange."

STREET VIEWS OF SOUTH BROADWAY

"You know me, Mayor Snyder, I got a big appetite to fill."

It's true—the Fat Man probably spends more on my dinners than he does on my girls, and that's saying something.

"So you boys got any ideas who's backing her?" I asked.

"No word down at the hall—copper boys don't seem to know—" said Pinky.

"—or be paid off on high," the Fat Man interrupted.

I snorted aloud, "Chief Freeman—that blind pig. He wouldn't know what to do with the information if I fed it to him."

Pinky nodded his head in agreement. "So you know who it is, then?"

"Won't be long before I do. Ain't no way all those girls are satisfied working for that woman."

The Fat Man raised his glass. "Always ten steps ahead, Pearl."

We drained the last drops of the whiskey, and then I headed back to the house, the warmth from the liquor doing little to dull my irritation. I'll tell you, that girl's got it coming—mucking up my head so I can't even enjoy my ride through my empire tonight. Usually it's my favorite part of the day, when my cabman blows his trumpet as we roll along Spring Street, announcing my arrival as I wave to my subjects in front of Childs' Opera House. My white bulldog, Pat, sits proudly on my lap, and a couple of my top strumpets, on either side of me, tilt their parasols and wink at the regulars. Advertising.

But tonight I ride alone. Gotta remind this town who I am.

In my business you gotta stay ahead of the sport, always be providing new niceties 'n' entertainment. Threw a ball just last week. It cost me a hundred and fifty dollars for the invites alone—gilt lettered on embossed cream paper. Had them hand-delivered to my top fifty customers and the new members of the Los Angeles Athletic Club as a welcome gift. Some of their fathers have had accounts with me since they paved the streets with cement back in the early '80s.

You want to stay fresh in this business, you got to be constantly diversifying your pussy.

My most popular sport is my cherry auctions. I only extend those invites to my highest-paying guests. Gotta earn that spot. I get the pick of the crop for my festivities—plenty of unwanted children who've grown too old to be babied. Girl's gonna be a stale virgin if she keeps it too long.

You wouldn't believe what they'll pay for a girl who is innocent. They all like the fantasy of breaking her in, even if their neighbors think they had the privilege. I even offer a maidenhood inspection by my house physician, Dr. Charles William Bryson. He provides certificates of authenticity. Gotta keep an eye on ol' Diamond Tooth Charlie, that lousy lush. Likes to test them out for himself.

Nothing riles up my customers like those auctions. Talk is hard on an average night—men speak freely among themselves about their sporting pursuits. But on the evenings when fresh blood is proffered, the comments I record in the early morning hours reach a fever pitch.

———

"Thank god for the service of women."

"A woman could occupy seventy men all night long
to save a country (a man is spent after one)."

"I don't want to take my shoes off;
I like it spontaneous and dirty."

"You need a long tongue to reach the honeypot."

"Walk like you've been properly fucked
(you don't have to fight this like a virgin, you know)."

"They have to have long hair so we have something to pull."

"I rode her hard and put her away wet . . ."

———

Finding fresh meat's on my mind as I ride through the darkening streets of my fair city. Why, just Thursday morning I was down at the orphan asylum with the Fat Man on his rounds, looking. He's one of their most generous patrons. He likes to ensure that he's getting his money's worth. Pays me double to procure one of those tenderfeet for him back at my house.

We walked right through those iron gates like we owned the asylum. Mother Superior Cecilia had the girls march out single file and line up in front of us. The Fat Man strolled the line a few paces in front of me, giving me a nudge when he found one worthy of closer inspection. In the middle of the second row he stopped in front of a dirty little moppet—matted brown hair hanging all over her face, eyes trained to the floor, arms folded behind her back. We stood together, appraising the little bastard. The Fat Man took her chin in one pudgy hand and lifted the child's face up for a better look. He turned her cheeks this way and that, as if selecting an orange, using saliva on his fingertips to wipe a smudge from her brow. The girl closed her eyes at the touch of his spit.

I had the fear too. The first time. But a girl's gotta make a living. She can't be a burden on society.

The girl looked right at me as we stood there, considering. Pleading with those big eyes. I almost felt sorry for her. I leaned in to sniff the top of her head. Head lice. A lot of dirty bastards, they were. Row by row, the whole lot.

Gotta scrub 'em up good before showing them to the customers. It's a damn tiring job, I'll tell you—a woman's work is never done.

Between you and me I could use a lie-down myself. Hell, I'm just shy of sixty now—ain't saying which side—and I always said sex was a young person's business. I must've aged forty years in the first six months alone back on the ranch. But those were different times. Customers didn't expect all the bells and whistles they do now in a proper house. Back then a girl could get by on what's between her legs alone.

STREET VIEWS OF
South Broadway

South Broadway
MERCANTILE PLACE

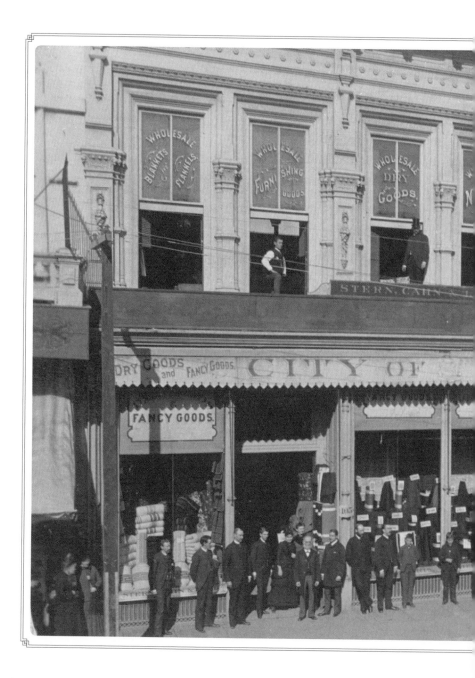

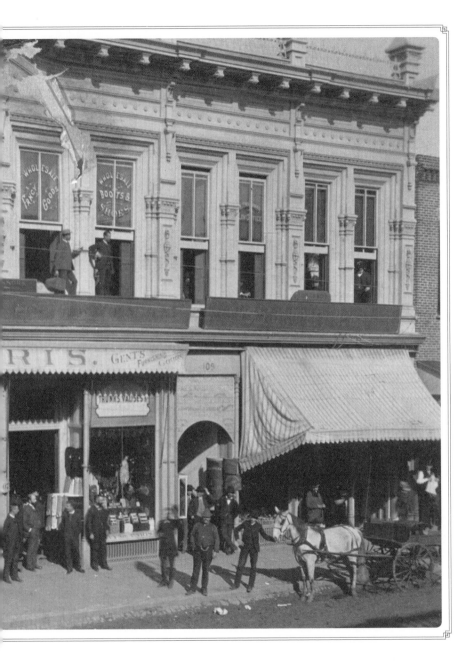

City of Paris

1890 Spring Street

Sometimes I get to thinking about retiring, get myself an ostrich ranch—those feathers cost me enough at the milliner's. Got a robust pension saved down at the bank and enough stock in stolen confidences to cash in. Always wanted to visit Europe. Certainly earned it after all these years.

Pasadena
Ostrich Farm

But I don't know what else I'd do. I really ain't much cut out for any other trade, and I've worked too damn hard for too long to give up my throne just yet. I'll tell you one thing, though, that girl Cora Phillips had better watch her back. 'Cause I sure as Satan ain't going out without a fight.

Ostrich Feather Stoles

Black, White or Any Color

Probably in no other form are ostrich feathers developed to produce a more charming effect than in the fashionable Stole. This article is formed of two or more strands of ostrich feathers invisibly joined together to form a broad, flat effect, each strand being in reality a miniature Boa. Our Stoles are carefully made of strong, vigorous stock, most beautifully curled, and always prove satisfactory to the wearer. **For natural colors see page 11.**

No. 2025, 2 yards, 2 strands..$20.00

No. 2535, 2 yards, 3 strands.. 25.00

No. 2527, 2½ yards, 2 strands 25.00

No. 3029, 3 yards, 2 strands.. 30.00

No. 5039, 3 yards, 3 strands.. 50.00

Ostrich Feather Muffs

The vogue of the Ostrich Feather Muff is rapidly increasing, and its popularity is most deserved, since it combines great beauty and warmth with no suggestion of the odor which is so pronounced in furs.

Cawston Ostrich Feather Muffs are most carefully made of select stock from male birds, and are handsomely lined with a fine quality satin.

Ostrich Feather Muff, satin lined, any shade, no tails......$30.00

Ostrich Feather Muff, satin lined, four tails, any shade.... 35.00

Ostrich Feather Muff, best grade, four tails, any shade.... 40.00

A group of nurses on the lawn.
Identies unknown.

The orderlie is showing how one of the nurses
acted one night when he asked her to help him
carry out a corpse of a patient who had just
died.

CHAPTER TWO

SUICIDE AT PEARL'S

It was reported that an inmate of Pearl Morton's house, Freda Clifford, attempted suicide last night. She was taken to the hospital after swallowing three strychnine tablets in a glass of whiskey. She left the following note:

> *My parents endeavored to bring us up in the fear*
> *and admonition of the Lord . . . we were to walk in*
> *the path of virtue . . . to bear up all the trials of the*
> *world even till . . . at the age of thirteen I left my*
> *parents to come live with Dr. W. For trying to avoid*
> *the wicked design of my master, I was pushed down*
> *stairs and many unmentionable horrors I lived*
> *through . . . I had to follow the works of darkness . . .*
> *guilty of the great sin of self-destruction, which I*
> *would have done long ago if not for the words of*

that noble gentleman Mr. —, who set me up in fine
house . . . but oh what horrors would these words
pierce my heart . . . tempted by Satan . . . convinced
of my lost and sinful state, I kneel . . . day and
night, I have cried unto the Lord to turn my wicked
heart to fly from hell to rise . . . the day of grace falls
fast away all things done before the circuit of the
sun . . . with shame I own, I return to thee, Lord. . . .
there is no place left to go . . . repentance is mine. . . .
what will become of my soul?

CHAPTER THREE

DRUG ADDICTION

Oh, but what terrible boredom afflicts the ladies of the house, as they wait for the evening's clients to arrive. Weary souls wasting away hours indoors as the sun fades away, prepping themselves for the onslaught of men. An interval of time before their bodies will be bought and sold. Used up. Likely dead by the time they are forty. It is no wonder that many prostitutes take laudanum drops or morphine to dull their response to pain and pass the time between bedfellows.

These magical drops come all the way from China. It is the peak of the opium trade, and morphine and opium alkaloids are readily available in Los Angeles by the late 1880s. At least a dozen opium dens operate in Chinatown alone.[1] Several dens

---

1. According to Horace Bell, crusader against corruption and publisher

are even listed on the Dakin fire insurance maps of the era.[2]

Prescribed by doctors, uterine wafers containing morphine can be inserted into the vagina for irregular or painful menstruation. Laudanum is tax free if approved as a medicine; even society women use it to achieve their ideal facial pallor.

For whores and polite ladies alike, nerve tonics are promoted to control "neurasthenia"—a condition whose symptoms include anxiety attacks, hysteria, exhaustion, depression, and headaches—thought to afflict most women "particularly in the higher circles of society, where their emotions are over-educated and their organization delicate."[3] Mrs. Winslow's Soothing Syrup, a

---

of a newspaper, *The Porcupine*, from 1882 to 1888, which detailed vice in Los Angeles.

2. See map, pages x-xi.

3. George H. Napheys, A.M., M.D., *The Physical Life of Woman: Advice to the Maiden, Wife and Mother* (Philadelphia: H.C. Watts Co., 1878).

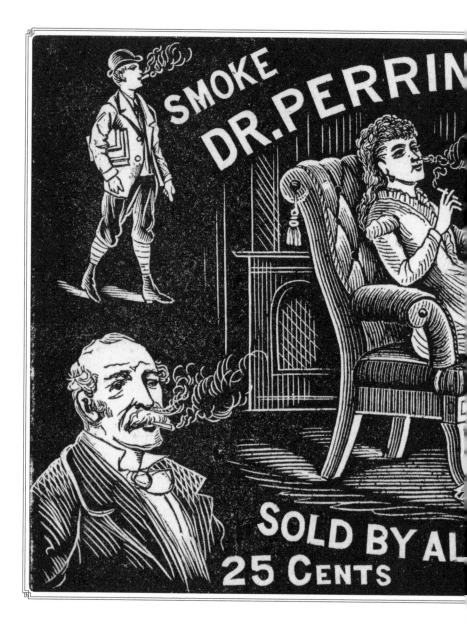

Smoke cigarettes for health

mixture of opium and brandy, and Godfrey's Cordial, containing high amounts of morphine, are both sold over the counter. A wide variety of medicinal "bitters" are little more than "lures to drunkenness."[4] The popular Boker's Stomach Bitters has an alcohol content of 42.6 percent.[5]

Private physicians and brothel-house doctors prescribe stronger tinctures for insomnia, in the form of pure morphine or laudanum in mysterious dark glass bottles. These can be found in many a woman's boudoir, or alongside the bodies of prostitutes who have committed suicide in Los Angeles's sporting houses.

---

4. City Document No. 85, Third Annual Report of the Board of Health of the City of Boston, 1875.

5. For comparison's sake, beer contains between 2% and 8% alcohol.

Not tonight, dear. I have a headache.

CHAPTER FOUR

CORA PHILLIPS

I am a slave to my master.
He who keeps me.
On his clock.
By his whims.
On his dime.
Even inside my own home I am not free.

Though I am madam, it is X who truly rules my house. And he does so with an iron heart and a heavy fist. His eyes are on me everywhere—via the secret passageways he built to run behind every room—so that he could conduct his all-consuming re-search in anonymity. Most nights he creeps along these darkened corridors, watching from the wings like a scientist observing his specimens. Behind composed lips, his tongue flicks, his mouth waters, surveying his game.

Even now, when the light outside is still golden and he is asleep miles away, I can feel him in every corner, at every turn. Always watching.

I used to be comforted knowing I had a protector. But now I am as trapped as the grasshopper sparrow locked up in the birdcage that hangs in the front window of the house. A discreet signal to customers: when the cage is uncovered, we are open for business. Like every thread of the web that ensnares me, X designed the house with such exacting details, evident only to the most discerning eye.

Besides the girls, whom I've carefully chosen and groomed, X personally hired all the house staff, the better to keep an eye on his business. He's allowed me one ally, my butler, Emerson, whom I brought with me from England. Emerson ensures that I have some modicum of privacy. I leave him to handle all the public aspects of running the house, sending him out in my stead to do the house banking, to retrieve my sundries and my medicine. And it is he who greets gentleman callers at the front door, directing them to wait patiently in the foyer while their calling cards are brought to my drawing room. Only a chosen few are summoned upstairs for further examination of wallets and credentials. I prefer to keep my customers at a distance. I have been propositioned myself too many times.

Once a house account has been opened, Emerson shows our customer to the main receiving parlor, lush and formal, where my ladies lounge in evening attire, satin dancing slippers on their feet. The draperies, a soothing cream and pale blue silk, hang in deep folds. Hand-painted scenes on the walls depict pastoral settings. Upon closer inspection, one can see small figures in the landscape, men and women engaged in various sex acts. X had made note of something similar in the brothels of Pompeii.

The east side of the room features sliding plate glass doors that open into a medium-size ballroom, furnished with gold chairs set against the walls and a grand piano in the corner. Louis, my piano player, is on retainer. Maids in starched aprons serve drinks. In the well-stocked wine cellar in the basement, favored clients are allowed to house their own vintages.

There is plenty of money to waste in this town.

On the second floor is a formal dining room, where my ladies eat a light supper together before starting work. They complete their shifts with a late dinner before retiring for their well-deserved beauty sleep.

Next to the dining room is a grand private bathroom appointed with a large tub in the middle of the room. The walls are lined with mirrors, and the floor is set with black and white marble tiles X had imported from Venice. On Sundays, the ladies bathe in fresh milk.

The bathroom serves another purpose, as several customers enjoy being urinated on—a request I would prefer not to satisfy in my house. But as X reminds me, we aim to fulfill all manner of fantasy. The tub is his concession to confine these acts to clean water.

Adjoining the grand bathroom is a wardrobe room, where the girls are fitted for their "uniforms." As well as a full-time dress-maker, I keep a house physician, Dr. Perskin, on staff. My girls are given weekly checkups, even though they are always spot-less. I believe we are the only house that insists that all gentle-men wear prophylactics. X imports them from France in sealed packets bearing the house's stamp: The Golden Lion.

In the receiving salon, maids whisper discreetly to their mistresses when their rooms are cleared of the previous guest, and if so inclined, the gentleman and his lady retire upstairs. The girls' private quarters are as sumptuous as the public rooms. We have brass monkeys on pulls by each bed to summon the chamber-maid. Our kitchen is kept busy all night, as scullery and upstairs maids come and go, carrying refreshments and fresh linens.

It takes great effort and staff to maintain the high level of excel-lence expected from my house. Though I am highly selective of my stable of ladies, it's proven imperative, in this city without manners, to educate the girls on proper etiquette. I personally tutor them in the arts of conversation and toilette. One could say my house is a finishing school for lowborn ladies. I've found graciousness to be a woman's best asset, even in the vilest cir-cumstances.

I keep a strict set of house rules, which is given to every girl inside a small leather book. The book includes blank pages for the girls to make notes on their clients' preferences. They fill their pages with tricks and lore, recipes for lemon juice and whiskey, to keep the wares in working order. One must note what was tried and what has failed.

And they trade notes on those to avoid—ones whose desire, unhinged, comes loose with violent results, if not restrained with proven methods for taming. Or others with nerves to soothe, eager to prove their range. And then the very young, usually their favorites, so full of wonder, ready to please, willing to try, on bended knee—their purses flung open, spilling forth golden treasures.

I wander the secret hallways of my house as X does, each day before dusk, making sure my guidelines are adhered to. I stand quietly in the shadows, studying the last rays of sunlight dotting the plush Turkish carpeting lining my ladies' boudoirs, admiring the perfect interiors he designed after many years of study—a chaise lounge in the middle of the room, strewn with pillows, and vanities set with all the accoutrements of a toilette.

And now my highest-earning girl, Velvet Ass Rose, sits in front of the mirror, readying herself. She looks weary, spent before the first customer arrives, slumping on the vanity as her chambermaid, Dolly, performs the nightly ritual of lacing her corset, pushing one

———

1. Matching brassieres and blouses

2 Hair combed and in place

3 Light rouging

4 Baths twice daily, no exceptions

5 Prompt for mealtimes

6 No inter-inmate affairs

7. No foul language

8 No Laudanum or Opiate use

———

foot against Velvet's back, both hands pulling with force. The stays will only be carelessly undone by fumbling hands later. Velvet's eyelids droop and close as Dolly blathers on about the evening's guests:

"Well, Mr. J, he's sure to be in top form tonight—comin' straight from his daughter's engagement party. . . . I imagine he'll have had a few toffs by now. He'll be on a red-hot rip tonight! Oooh, I do hope he brings his son with him. Junior is coming along so nicely—sixteen, perfect age—about time his father opened an account for him here. Can't be a mama's boy much longer or he'll join those fairy messenger boys."

"Mind your mouth and focus," Velvet mutters.

"Such airs this evening, Miss Velvet, you'd think you was getting a bit high-and-mighty if I didn't—"

A knock at the door breaks into Dolly's chatter. Velvet lifts her head slowly, her eyelids heavy.

"Yes?"

The door opens a crack as my maid, Josephine, peeks in. X brought her from England too, to make sure I was well attended in my own boudoir.

"It's Miss Cora, she requires to see you in her study."

"I'm comin'," Velvet drawls.

"Wonder what you did now, Miss Velvet, summoned all official-like by the mistress."

"Shut up and do your job. I don't have all night to listen to your nonsense."

Dolly rushes to finish, tying the bottom laces into a small bow and then hands Velvet a pink silk evening robe with an embroidered Asian motif before withdrawing. With the door safely shut, Velvet pulls out a small, folded-up piece of paper tucked between her breasts. She reads its lines and smiles to herself, then folds the paper back up again, pushing it deep inside her cleavage. My girls think they can keep confidences. But no such secrets can be kept in my house. My master taught me well.

Velvet Ass Rose. My wild, imperfect thoroughbred. Said she'd mind the rules, no tales or lies, but I know that she has been taking notes for Pearl Morton, who runs her own house over on Marchessault Street. Competition is fierce in this town, and my arrival ten months ago has threatened Pearl's reign. I know there is a price on my head, though no one will tell me that to my face.

Velvet's espionage is worthless—the girl knows only what I allow her to; it's rather easy to feed fabricated intelligence to an easy mark. Should she find out anything useful, X would put a stop to it before I could. Regardless, I really don't care to engage in petty rivalries—Pearl could have it all for the taking, my house, my girls, my customers—if X would only let me.

From my perch in the corridor, looking in through a small hole in the oil painting that hangs above her bed, I gaze at Velvet. She takes a small horsehair brush and dips it into a pot of rouge, making circles around each already rosy nipple. Her lips turn up in a smirk, enjoying her smugness. A last hairpin to secure her chignon and she is ready to face me.

It is my cue to withdraw quietly, turn left back down the darkened corridor and up my private staircase to my drawing room to await her arrival.

I instruct Josephine to delay Velvet's entrance, knowing it will try Velvet's patience. She must learn that it is a virtue in this business. I take a moment to collect myself in front of my looking glass.

My skin is pale, my dark brown hair twisted into a low bun at the nape of my neck and my cheeks pink from the overheated room. I keep a fire lit at all hours so that it reminds me of England, even in this dry heat.

Unlike my ladies' dishabille, I wear a high-necked blouse in a stiff cream silk. I've learned that what is hidden is more desired than what is on show. All men like a challenge. My only concession to extravagance is a brooch pinned to my breast—a miniature painting of an eye, surrounded by tiny pearls. Except for that, I wear no other jewelry, nor do I wear paint.

I make my way to a large desk at the far end of the room and sit down in front of my red leather account book—it is almost as large as the span of my own arms. In such confrontations, I cultivate an impression of great seriousness to appear older than my twenty-nine years. No one likes a dressing-down, much less from a woman barely old enough to run a house like mine properly.

There is a knock at the door.

"Come in, please."

Velvet enters and I motion for her to sit before me, which she does with calculated insolence, certain of my displeasure.

"Velvet . . ."

"Yes, Madam Cora."

"It has come to my attention that you have flagrantly disregarded the rules yet again."

"It's not true! Who said so?"

I produce a small glass bottle with a cork stopper from the top drawer of my desk and set it on the table. Velvet's face falls, her eyes narrowing in anger.

"Was it that Dolly snooping in my room?!"

"This was found during tidying yesterday evening. It was under your bed."

"It's for my monthlies. I have so much pain."

"Dr. Perskin will bring you Mrs. Winslow's Soothing Syrup on his rounds tonight; we've already discussed it."

"But—"

"Velvet. You have intelligence and some degree of charm. But if you wish to continue to work for me and live in the manner to which you've become accustomed . . ."

I pause, gesturing toward Velvet's silk kimono and velvet slippers.

"I do, Madam Cora."

"Then you must follow the standards I have set. I am not in this business to support a pack of street whores. I know of no other madam who allows her girls such liberties and luxuries. If you find yourself unhappy in my house, perhaps you should go and work for Pearl Morton."

Velvet's pink cheeks turn a deeper shade of crimson. She does not lift her gaze from the floor to meet my eyes.

"Are we clear?"

Velvet reluctantly nods her agreement. "Yes, Madam Cora."

Before I can dismiss her, we are interrupted by a quiet tap at the door, and then Emerson enters.

"Excuse me, Madam Cora, there's a young man to see you. He's here about Mrs. McDougal's request."

"Oh, is that scheduled for this evening? I've hardly had time to sort the details."

"No, madam, I've arranged it for tomorrow afternoon. But this young gentleman looks promising. I am sure Mrs. McDougal will approve."

"Very well, let's engage Rose to accompany."

"Very good, Madam Cora."

"Thank you, Emerson. You may show him in; we are finished here."

Emerson half bows to me, exiting to take care of my caller. The particulars I must attend to are endless, to serve my customers' diverse requirements.

"Madam Cora?"

"Yes, Velvet?" I had already dismissed her from my mind.

"I almost forgot. I got a message for you. From my afternoon client—you know?"

My heart drops. I can feel the blood drain from my cheeks. But my face remains impassive. "I have a message," I correct her and then nod for her to continue.

"Well, he said he'd see me next Tuesday."

I nod again, relieved. Make a notation in my red ledger.

"Is that all?"

"And that he'll be around later to see you."

I speak carefully as my nails dig into my palms underneath my desk. "Good. That is all, Velvet, you may be excused."

Velvet mock-curtsies as she exits. "Very good, Madam Cora."

X would come tonight. It has been almost a fortnight since his last visit. I could just disappear. How many times I've wished to.

A desire for air overcomes me. Taking my cloak from my wardrobe, I exit through the small door hidden in a wall of books. Books are his obsession. They used to be mine.

The bookcase opens onto stairs that let out next to the front door. I draw the hood of my cloak low over my head and pause to cover the birdcage before I open the front door; the house will be temporarily closed for business.

I make my way to the back of the house toward a row of stables. I untie my stallion, Sweet Revenge, and mount quickly. With a gentle nudge, we are off, passing the stone lions guarding my house—brought over from England on the same steamer that delivered both me and my Sweet Revenge.

Dusk has fallen and the streets are quiet. I keep to the back alleys, avoiding the lamp-lit storefronts along Broadway and Main Street. The best defense is to be the one who goes unseen.

We accelerate to a gallop, out and away from the city center, north toward the grassy plains and brick mansions of Pasadena.

My thoughts come in a rush, wrapped up in the rhythm of hooves on the mud beneath. Memories of England come in flickering images as I ride.

An infant left on the doorstep of a barren milliner's wife, a brooch pinned to her swaddling cloth—a tiny painted eye set in seed pearls and mounted in gold with the initials C.P. engraved on the back.

The stench of the Haymarket.

Lying in a basket on the shop floor, peering up at rows of feathers and spools of lace on shelves. Painted ladies placing orders for hats, petting my head with sad sighs. The smell of their lilac perfume, the sound of their heels tapping on the wooden floor.

Mr. Littleton, the bookseller down the lane. Tall volumes of leather lining the walls. Endless stacks. Quiet. An offer to sweep his floors in exchange for borrowing services. Peaceful moments lost in the pages of a distant land, hidden up in my attic room. Safe. Nothing terrible could ever happen among the perfect rows of spines, neatly arranged by subject and author.

A secret door in the back of the bookshop. Rows of books kept hidden for preferred clients: *Demonology and the Dark Arts; A Dictionary of Velvet Tongue;* Pierce Egan's *Real Life in London;* volumes of the erotic journal *The Pearl.* The darkness of men's souls filled my mind before my fifteenth birthday.

And then, a calling card with a single initial: X.

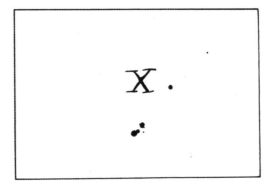

The most esteemed of Mr. Littleton's clients. I favored his orders over all the rest. In person, he mesmerized—rugged but handsome, deep lines in his features showing less age than distinction; eyes that shone with flecks of emerald green and were as cold as the gemstone; shiny brown hair curling past his ears, badly in need of a trim and a wash—disheveled but nonetheless charming.

He had a strange smile, his lips curling up at the corners into a smirk, teasing with all the secrets behind his eyes. He stood with studied insolence, one leg cocked, the other long and erect. He spoke with an air of indifference, every word chosen to intrigue.

With utter nonchalance he seduced me.

An offer to receive the finest education at his hands. To be molded into his perfect Pygmalion, his treasured protégée. My schools were Europe's best brothels.

No more girlish thoughts of love, of romance, of the sweet stirrings of youth. Stuck in the life he'd created for me, his fantasies my new reality.

Only once did I rise to the surface of this murky haze and taste life. A boy with dark hair tumbling over dark eyes waking me from my sleepwalking with love songs and broken promises. I can still feel his mouth on my neck, his breaths between my thighs. . . .

I jerk my head forcefully, to shake off visions too painful to allow. And then, riding hard, I am back. Here in this city I loathe. Spending endless days locked indoors against the blazing heat, a prisoner in my own home.

London was a second skin, I could roam the streets undisturbed, blend into the bustle of crowded cobblestone alleys. Los Angeles is all wide-open sunlit spaces—to venture outdoors here is to be exposed.

I feel like a ghost, floating through empty streets with no one seeing me. I peer out of curtained windows, watching gentlewomen strolling with their children in broad daylight, and wish to trade places with them. I am an old lady before I am even a woman.

All day I long for the hours of retreat into sleep, breathing steadily, dozing childlike—that beautiful slumber wrapped around me keeping loneliness at bay. If only there was a way to hold onto its tenderness in my waking hours.

Well . . .

I do have one such magical potion.

In England other girls introduced me to a dream in the form of laudanum drops. Many of them were addicted. I resisted as long as my willpower would dare, but its pull was too great, its availability so ready, and the deep fog that rolled in was like no other seduction I had ever known.

Other girls passed the time with sapphic pleasures, but I couldn't rouse my desire to join them. It was easier with the customers, a straightforward transaction without any mess afterward. No declarations of romance nor shattered hearts. My surface remained impenetrable.

The drops were like a velvet touch. Soft fingers gently grazing each of my veins, stroking my skin, lulling me to sleep. I dreamt in vivid colors, obscure memories mixed with cerulean blue.

A permanent mist, lovely and gray. Cozy in my ineptitude— like lying about all day drinking tea, listening to the crunch of boots on gravel. Time at a standstill. The slightest breath on the windowpane, disappearing slowly. The great effort to transfer cold feet onto the stone floor.

And a warm sensation creeping over, soothing, like water enveloping skin in an overflowing tub. Gliding toward streams of sunlight imagined. Nothing to do but relax into the darkness, forever floating, directionless. Where nothing is judged, nothing is remembered, nothing is permanent.

I promised myself I wouldn't become like other girls, with their dull stares, glassy pupils, and bruised-violet under-eyes. I took drops just when the throbbing in my seams and the noise in my head got too much. Lately, though, the weight upon me grows into a burden only the drops can soothe. I wear my mother's brooch every day, as though it were a childhood blanket, protecting me. She who left me on that doorstep. As a comfort. I laugh, thinking of the folly of my reasoning.

But nothing can protect me from my master. Always watching.

I ride faster. Oh, if I could only lose my way, be a stranger in the streets, another shadow in the dark.

My lips and eyelids are wet with salty tears. My skin is radiant in the full moonlight, but my heart is black.

Several weeks, months go by . . . I cannot tell, the seasons do not change, the days are monotonous. I open for business, collect the money, count the hours until I can sleep. I hardly care anymore to keep up my expected routine. What can he take away from me if I have nothing left?

The sun beats down outside, but my bedroom is dark, the curtains drawn tight against the smallest crack of light. The door is locked from the inside. I lay facedown on my canopied bed, my arms dangling over the edge. My eyelids flutter; my mind in and out of consciousness. My limbs twitch.

I toss and turn, sheets twisted around me, hot and sticky.

But even the drops can't stop my phantasm from visiting: the tall, dark man.

Bail in $300

County Court,

County of Los Angeles.

*The People of the State of Califor-
nia, against*

Cora Doe

Indictment for *keeper*
House of ill fame

A TRUE BILL :

M. H. Kimball

Foreman of the Grand Jury.

*Presented by the Foreman of the
Grand Jury, in the presence of the
Grand Jury, in open County Court
of the County of Los Angeles, State
of California, and filed as a record
of said Court this . . . .*

. . . . . . 25th . . . . day of

. . . . Sept . . . . . . A. D. 1875

. . . . . Clerk.

*By . . . .
. . . . Deputy Clerk.*

*. . . . .
. . . . District Attorney.*

*F. H. Howard
Dep Dist Att*

Long hair obscures his face. Strong hands hold my wrists above my head. He is on top of me, over me, inside me. I moan aloud. I am awake, alive, pulsating. I feel him everywhere—even in between my eyes, piercing so intensely I fear my eardrums might burst. I scream but make no sound. His face moves closer to mine; his hair grazes my mouth. I open my eyes and look up at him. My pupils dilate, freezing in recognition as his features come into focus.

X. My pleasure and my torture.

I bolt upright in bed, gasping, perspiration dripping from my forehead. I reach toward my bedside table, knocking over the small dark glass bottle. I clutch it to my bosom, loosen the stopper, and slowly measure more drops onto my tongue.

Calmed, I sink into my pillows again with a long exhale and wait for the exquisite darkness to fall.

"Are you all right?"

A voice. A man's voice.

"Are you all right, Miss Phillips . . . Cora?"

My eyelids open with a great struggle. Every joint trembles and aches. A man sits on the edge of my bed. Dr. Perskin. But who had let him in here? As though answering my thoughts, he speaks.

"Emerson rang for me. You were screaming in your sleep, the door was locked . . ."

I look past him to the door, where Emerson is peering around the damaged hinges; at my stare he gazes at the floor sheepishly and then retreats.

"He said you hadn't left your room since Tuesday evening."

"What day is it?"

"Thursday afternoon."

"He shouldn't have troubled you."

"I was already doing my rounds. It's really my pleasure."

"I'm fine."

"Please, Miss Phillips, may I . . ."

His hands slide around my waist, against the small of my back, pulling me toward him firmly and lifting me upright. Propping a pillow behind my head, he lowers me into its folds. He gently wipes my forehead with a handkerchief from his breast pocket, then pauses, as though considering my features. He reaches toward me to push the matted hair from my forehead with his fingers. They are coarser than I'd expected.

But why do I anticipate his hands, his touch at all? I wish he wouldn't look at me so intently. With his deep blue eyes. I fold my arms around myself, in protection. I remember the bottle. What if he found it. . . . I glance at my nightstand; it wasn't there.

"Are you looking for this?"

He removes the dark glass bottle from inside his jacket, then puts it back.

"You shouldn't have come in here!"

His kind bedside eyes are filled with concern. "I understand."

"No you don't, you couldn't."

"I've seen a lot in this town, in your business. It must be difficult."

"What are you saying?"

He pauses, an uncomfortable silence. I can see him carefully choosing his words.

"Forgive me if I am being inappropriate, but may I ask you something?"

I already know what is coming, another secret I would have to pay to keep. I let out a long, even breath. "Yes?"

"How many lovers have you taken?"

It wasn't the question I had expected.

"A lady doesn't tell and a gentleman shouldn't ask."

"I see."

I meet his gaze and study his face. "I'm really all right, so you can take your leave. I don't need your assistance."

"Are you certain?"

"Quite."

Still, he sits a moment longer, moving his hand across the bed to touch my wrist softly. I cross my arms tighter. He understands, pulling his hand away from me. Hesitantly, he gets up to leave, pausing just before the door.

"I could help if you let me."

And he shuts it softly behind him as he leaves.

What a strange man. And his manner—at once soothing and provocative—quite unexpected from a man I'd dismissed so. It's unsettling to have had him see me in such a state.

I pull myself out of bed with determination and gingerly make my way across the room to my vanity. I look into my mirror, beyond my reflection, the ugliness of my demons in every feature. I wonder if he could see them too. I am broken, repulsed by the sight of myself.

My whole body shakes with a cold sweat, I am badly in need of another drop. But he has taken the bottle, the doctor. I can't stop thinking about the feel of his hands, even though I want to.

I appraise my likeness in the glass, then pin my hair into a bun, pinching my cheeks to bring some color. I take my brooch from its velvet-lined case and affix it at my throat. I open the bottom left drawer of my vanity and remove the bottle taped to the back. Take one last drop. With a last glance in the mirror, I am ready. Time to open for the night.

ERECTED BY THE WOMEN OF WOODCRAFT

WOMEN OF WOODCRAFT
COURAGE HOPE REMEMBRANCE

CORA MAY PHILLIPS
1872 – 1912
GONE BUT NOT FORGOTTEN

Grave rubbing, Angelus-Rosedale Cemetary.

Phillips's date of birth appears to be incorrect
as 1875 court records [page 65]
would have Cora arrested for running a
house of ill fame at age three.

CHAPTER FIVE

GHOST BRIDE

(Female client, special request. Recent widow.)

You just like to watch, huh?

She needed to forget.

She wished he wouldn't speak.

She took another swig.

He pushed the other girl aside, getting out of bed to approach her. Taking the champagne bottle from her hands, he swallowed a big gulp.

If you come back to bed, we don't have to talk at all.

He held the bottle back toward her lips, tipping it up so that she could take a sip. With his other hand, he untied the ribbons on her bloomers, dropping them to the floor. Cupping his hand between her legs, he twisted a short lock of her hair into a curl. She looked him in the eyes, a silent challenge. She took the bottle back from him with both hands and gulped the bubbly liquid. Slowly, he unbuttoned her chemise and slipped his hand inside, tracing her nipples with his fingertips. Her neck arched slightly.

That's a girl, c'mon now, let me take care of you, make you forget all about him.

She shook her head. He took the bottle back, frowning as he raised it to his lips—it was empty. Tossing it on the carpet, he led her by both hands to the bed, pushing her down onto it. The other girl, covered with a sheet, sat propped up against the pillows, watching. He knelt before the bed, parting her legs, picking up each one carefully, and placing them around his neck. He started to lick between her thighs.

No . . . I can't . . . I'm mourning my lost love.

He tilted his head up to look at the tears falling softly from her eyes. Her words had struck him in a place he kept hidden. He studied her face, trying to decide if she was telling the truth. Rising from his knees, he crawled on top of her, leaning his face close to hers to whisper, *Don't worry, he'll come back.*

I don't want him back.

A long silence as he pondered a response.

Don't worry, he won't come back to you.

He kissed her more fiercely, pinning her arms down, spreading her legs with his knees. Her body barely responded to his touch. Keeping her restrained, he licked her neck, breasts, belly, then finally let go to resume his position between her legs, running his tongue along her pale white thighs. She couldn't help but moan.

That's right, that a girl.

I can't ... enough ... stop ...

He continued lapping his tongue, biting her softly. She climaxed twice. He didn't let up.

No ... no ... yes ... no ... Stop ... no more ...

He poked his head up, wiping his mouth with the back of his hand. He watched her breasts rise and fall as she panted for breath. He clambered back into bed, preparing to mount her.

Ready for something different?

I can't ... I'm not ... not ready.

She had a million excuses.

She was exhausted by his desire to pleasure her. He was too eager. Her heart ached with the memories of the man she loved.

She pushed him off and onto the other girl. She got up to pace the room, taking another bottle of champagne from a bucket of ice near the door.

She watched for a while. Her body swayed back and forth to the sounds of a phonograph playing in the adjoining room. She drank the last drop. She was suddenly so tired. She just wanted to sleep.

She climbed back into bed, clutching the empty bottle to her heart. He was thrusting himself between the legs of the other girl, who moaned in increasing volume. She lay down next to them, cradling her bottle. Tears streaked her face. He flipped the other girl sideways on the bed so that the girl's back faced her own. He met her eyes and reached a hand across the other girl's body to clasp hers. The girl writhed. He grabbed her hair, squeezed her shoulder, and stared into her eyes as he emptied himself into the body of the girl between them.

Anatomical illustrations from The Ladies New Medical Guide, 1890

INTERNAL ORGANS OF CHEST AND PELVIS

CHAPTER SIX

SEXUALITY

Middle- and upper-class sexuality at the end of this century dictates constant dedication to etiquette. Women are expected to be modest, virtuous, maternal, and to keep a good home.

Thought of as the weaker sex, women are directed to dress for warmth and modesty in the bedroom, covering themselves from neck to ankle in gowns or woolen union suits while they sleep. During the day, they wear boned and laced corsets under their garments, accentuating a full bust and a wasp waist. Even while nursing a newborn, a maternity corset is advised. Layer upon layer of clothing restricts movement and removes women from their own bodies—clothing acts as a sort of chastity belt, protecting them from their sexual desires, and those of others.

Constrained in every sense, women are detached from the pleasures of making love, even with their spouse. Open expression of sexual feelings is considered indecent. "Moral" wives cultivate sexual remoteness. Physicians claim that most women are entirely frigid, with a tenth the sexual energy of men. Female orgasms ("voluptuous spasms") are said to interfere with conception; separate beds for spouses are advocated. Reproduction is the only virtuous reason a husband should lie with his wife.[6]

Gentlewomen are not allowed even the luxury of impure thoughts. Physicians and reformers urge women to steer clear of romance novels, lest reading them cause blood to flow to the sexual organs and induce excessive excitement. Only the most progressive women dare to openly flaunt such salacious reading material, even as others whisper about them in drawing rooms.

Regardless of propriety, there is a strong undercurrent of kink— *Venus in Furs*, the notorious novel celebrating sadomasochism by author Leopold Sacher-Masoch came out in 1870. The European sport of spanking has become very much the fashion behind closed doors in America, though generally not practiced between husband and wife.

---

6. "The great object of the conjugal union is the transmission of life —a duty necessary in order to repair the constant ravages of death, and thus perpetuate the race." Napheys, *The Physical Life of Woman.*

Glamour portrait

circa 1890

Unfinished Skirt Patterns.

These Skirt Patterns are put up in pieces just the right amount to make a skirt. They are sold at very close prices, and are listed by us for the benefit of those who have the time or inclination to do the work at home.

No. 23621 This is an All Wool Skirt Pattern, of ample material to make a skirt of any size wanted. Comes in red and black, blue and black, or gray and black, with narrow and wide stripes. We can furnish it in plain brown if desired. Comes full 40 inches wide. It is made of very choice quality of material, and after the skirt is made up at home, it would equal anything that you could secure at a retail store at $1.50 to $2.00.
Our special price, per pattern..................**69c**

No. 23622 This is an All Wool, Strictly Non-Shrinkable Skirt Pattern. It is very closely woven, and is a quality that is very durable and warm. Comes in red and black, blue and black, or grey and black, with narrow and wide stripes.
Our special price, per pattern..................**78c**

No. 23623 This is an extra quality, very fine All Wool Skirt Pattern, and we can furnish it in a variety of combinations, such as blue and black, red and black, or black and white, with narrow and wide stripes; or, if so desired, we can furnish it in large checks. This skirt after made up would equal anything your local dealer would ask $2.00 for.
Our special price..................**95c**

No. 23624 We offer a very excellent quality of Mixed Flannel Skirting, with neat woven border of same goods in stripes. This when made up makes an exceedingly warm and durable skirt. The goods are all closely woven stuff, and we consider the pattern one of the choicest bargains we offer.
Our special price, per pattern..................**90c**

CORSET DEPARTMENT.

A Corset Weighs about 15 Ounces.

Our efforts to make the corset department one of the foremost departments of our vast establishment have not been in vain. We now sell several thousands of corsets weekly. Taking care to sell nothing but good corsets that we can guarantee, no matter how low the price, and at all times selling corsets at prices way down, has built up our business in this line.

We directly control the manufacture of a great many of the corsets we sell, and are in a position to see that the material is good, the fit perfect and the corset durable.

If you want to buy one Corset as cheap as your local dealer buys one or more dozens, send your order to us, Sears, Roebuck & Co.

Please order corsets by waist measure only. Corsets are numbered by actual waist measure. If measure is taken outside of dress, deduct two inches for dress, and this will give you the correct size to order. Do not order by bust measure.

Dr. Warner's Four-in-Hand Corsets

No. 23631 Boned with Coraline. High Hip for ladies with large hips whose corsets break down at the sides. Just the corset for such people. It is worth four times the price to any one so troubled. It is easy fitting and adds grace to the figure. Comes in drab only. Sizes 18 to 30. Per pair..................**75c**

Warner's 333 Corset.

No. 23632 Boned with Coraline. Extra long waist, medium form. A very popular corset, made of heavy jean with three boned strips of fine sateen. Beautifully shaped and a very comfortable, easy fitting corset. Colors drab or black. Sizes 18 to 30.
Price..................**75c**

Dr. Warner's Health Corset.

Boned with Coraline.
No. 23633 Made in Two Lengths, medium and long waist; adapted to ladies deficient in bust fullness, and those desiring bust support. For both slim and stout figures. The special features of this corset are the Coraline busts, which are light and flexible, and give to any lady an elegant figure, and assure a well fitting dress. This corset, with constant improvements, has been before the public for seventeen years, and has been worn by over six millions of ladies, a success never attained by any other corset. Colors; white, drab or black. Sizes 18 to 30. Price..................**$1.00**

No. 23634 Extra Long Waist 6 Hook Corset made of the best quality satin handsomely embroidered, a corset that will give satisfaction and one of the best corsets that we handle; drab or black.
Price, per pair..................**90c**

BALL'S STYLE B.

No. 23635 The Most Comfortable Corset Ever Made. They need no "breaking in," has a coiled wire elastic section which yields to every movement of the wearer. Ball's corsets are boned with Kabo, made of fine quality jean; white and drab only.
Sizes 18 to 30.
Price..................**75c**
Extra sizes 31 to 36. Price..................**$1.00**

KABO STYLE 110.

No. 23636 A Corset of Perfect Form that will not stretch, break, roll up or pucker; extra long waist; made in white, French drab and black sateen. Sizes 18 to 30. Price..................**75c**
Extra sizes 31 to 36.
Price..................**$1.00**

Kabo Style 110

NOTE—If you require a corset larger than size 30, order from those we quote in extra sizes. Ordinary corsets are made in sizes 18 to 30 only.

Dr. Warners' Coraline Corsets.

No. 23637 Made in Medium Length Waists. Adapted to ladies of average figure. This corset has been before the public for fifteen years, has the largest sale and gives the best value and best service of any dollar corset ever manufactured. Made in two thicknesses of fine corset jean, heavily boned with coraline in a manner that prevents the corset from losing its shape, and makes it absolutely unbreakable. The hip is extra stayed with clock spring side steels. Colors; drab or black. Sizes 18 to 30.
Price..................**$0.75**
Extra large sizes, 22 to 30, 25 cents extra.

Dr. Warners' Abdominal Corset.

No. 23638 Boned with Coraline. Adapted to ladies with either full or slender figure desiring a corset long below the waist, to give abdominal support. Made with extension steels, side lacings and elastic gores on each side. Colors; drab or black. Sizes 18 to 30.
Price..................**$1.25**
Extra large sizes, 31 to 36 inches. Each..................**$1.50**

Special Sewing Machine Catalogue Free.

Nursing Corset.

No. 23639. Nursing Corset. The most sensible, convenient and comfortable nursing corset made, well stayed on the sides, but very pliable over the sensitive parts of the body; the opening permits the escape of nipple without the least inconvenience; made of fine jean. Colors, white or drab; size, 18 to 30. Price..................**85c**

No. 23641 Ladies' Perfection Waist; made of fine sateen; soft puffed busts; clasp front. Colors white, black or drab. Sizes 18 to 30.
Price..................**90c**

No. 23642 Young Ladies' Corsets, suitable for girls 13 to 17 years of age; made of good jean; nicely corded; Colors, white or drab; sizes 18 to 26 waist measure. This corset in appearance and durability is equal to goods that retailers sell at a very much higher figure. Each..................**40c**

No. 23644 Warner Corsets, No. 65. Boned with husk proof, made of fine corset jean striped with sateen. The busts flexible, but sufficiently rigid to give form to the figure. Silk embroidered white, drab or black.
Price..................**75c**

No. 23646 Best Quality Jean Corset, striped with sateen, bone bust, two side steels, 6-hook clasp, embroidered at top and bottom; in shape, appearance and durability equal to any $1.00 corset; unquestionably the best corset ever produced for the money we ask. Colors; white, drab or black..................**50c**

No. 23648 Exposition, perfectly shaped and a fine fitting Corset, equal to any retailed at 80c; made of heavy jean, striped with sateen, wide zone, double bust, two side steels. Colors; white, drab, cream or gold..................**40c**

TENNIS AND CROQUET SETS AT POPULAR LOW PRICES IN SPORTING GOODS DEPARTMENT. REFER TO INDEX.

No. 23649 A Stiff High Bust Corset, with shoulder straps; made of fine quality sateen. This corset is especially intended for ladies with small bust dimensions. Colors, white and drab. Price. 90c

No. 23650 This Corset is modeled after the finest French shapes and will fit any lady of average proportions; it is made with soft busts and stayed with unbreakable French wire. Colors, black or drab. Size 18 to 30. Price........75c

No. 23651 Comfort and elegance, a summer corset made of improved netting; striped with satin; reinforced front steels, two side steels, and extra heavy back wire; six hook clasp; as perfectly fitting as any of the highest price corsets. Colors: white or drab; size 18 to 30. Price.................45c

No. 23652 A well made summer corset, with double bust; two side steels; wide zone; in white only; size 18 to 30. Price.................39c

No. 23653 French Coutel Corset; extra long waisted; sateen striped; fitted with unbreakable French wire; trimmed with handsome silk embroidery and heavily flossed, and produces an elegant appearance equaled only by corsets costing double the money. Colors: White, drab or black. Sizes, 18 to 30 only. Price............95c. Extra size in black only; size 31 to 36. Price........... $1.20

No. 23654 The Very Latest Improved French Corset, very highest grade workmanship and material; made of finest Zanella cloth, extra long waisted, medium size bust and hips, cross boned, high back, beautifully embroidered and finished in every way equal to any corset retailing for $2.65 each; colors, drab or black; size, 18 to 30........$1.89

No. 26655 High Grade Special Corset, in every way equal to the best imported corset that retails for $2.70; made of the best quality improved sateen, long waisted, high back, extra heavy clasp, elegantly embroidered and silk trimmed. Colors: white, drab or black; sizes 18 to 30..............$1.35

No. 23656 Ball's Child's Waists, with patent tape buttons and buttonholes; sizes, 18 to 28. A perfect fitting waist; colors white and drab. Price..........38c

No. 23657 Ball's Misses' Waist, white and drab; sizes, 18 to 28. Ball's waists are unequalled by any others in the market. Price.............55c

No. 23658.

No. 23658 Yong Ladies' Corset, with soft expanding bust; made of fine sateen with shoulder straps; clasp front; tape fastened buttons for skirt. Colors: white, drab or black; sizes, 19 to 28 waist measure; just the corset for growing girls 75c

No. 23659 Corset waist for girls from 8 to 12 years old; button front; lace back; made of fine quality silesia; well corded; shoulder straps; tape fastened buttons for skirts. Colors: white or drab; size 19 to 28...................69c

No. 23659.

No. 23660. Bust Pads, the kind that usually sell for 50 cents. Our price.....................25c

No. 23662. Ladies' Genuine Haircloth Combination Hip Pad Bustle, padded with curled hair, very light in weight, comes in black, drab and white, the usual retail price, $1.00. Our price, each....................56c

Ladies' White Skirts.

Lengths 36, 38, 40, 42 inches. Our skirts are three yards around the bottom, never less, often wider. Please give size when ordering.

No. 23670 Ladies' White Muslin Skirt, lawn ruffle 6½ inches wide, trimmed with embroidery, good width, patent facing. Each...$0.50 2 for .... .95 3 for.... 1.40

No. 23671 Muslin Skirt, umbrella style, 3 yards around bottom, lawn ruffle 6¾ inches wide finished with fine linen torchon lace, a regular $1.00 skirt. Each 65; 2 for $1.25; 3 for....................$1.85

No. 23672 Ladies' White Umbrella Skirt, 3 yards around bottom, lawn ruffle 6½ inches wide finished with open work embroidery, a regular $1.25 skirt. Each.....$0.79; 2 for...... 1.52 3 for...... 2.20

No. 23673 Ladies' White Skirt made of good muslin, 3 yards wide, 3 lawn ruffles 4½ inches wide, finished with torchon lace. 3 inches wide. Retailers ask $1.50 for goods like these. Each 90c; 2 for $1.70; 3 for $2.50

No. 23674 Ladies' Fine White Skirt, 3½ yards wide, has 9-inch lawn ruffle finished with very handsome open work embroidery; regular price $2.00. Each, $1.25. 2 for.... 2.40 3 for.... 3.30

No. 23675 A very Handsome Ladies' Skirt of good quality, 3½ yards wide. 16-inch lawn ruffle, finished with fine Hamburg embroidery; well worth $2.50 Each......$1.65 2 for........ 3.10 3 for........ 4.50

No. 23676 An exceptionally fine white underskirt for ladies. Umbrella pattern, 3¼ yards wide. English open work embroidery; width of ruffle and embroidery 15 inches. This skirt is well worth $3.75. Each, $1.85 2 for.... 3.50 3 for.... 5.00

.. SPECIAL BABY CARRIAGE CATALOGUE FREE ..

1890 Sears, Roebuck & Co. Catalogue

The "solitary vice" (masturbation) is considered a great danger. Social reformers and religious leaders warn of the evils associated with giving in to such instincts. There is little relief for legions of frustrated, undersexed housewives. But there are signs of change. At last, physical exercise for women has come into vogue, the most popular new sport being bicycle riding. Here too are countless rules for decorum, such as *"It is not strictly correct for a young lady to ride unaccompanied. . . . The unmarried woman who cycles must be chaperoned by a married woman. . . . Neither must the married woman ride alone."*[7] Still, the ability to ride outside in the fresh air offers a reprieve for repressed women.

Men, with their "natural" sexual urges, need to find release elsewhere. Contemporary "smut" magazines and sporting weeklies like New York's *Flash* and *The Whip* offer some stimuli and are available throughout the country. Prostitution serves a large portion of the male population aching to satiate its sexual appetites outside the marital contract. Across cities and in small towns all over America, whores are available at every price. And what a welcome sight these women are, with their loose bloomers, easy sensuality, and total disregard for social convention. Men are expected to feel contempt for the women who administer to their lust, sanctifying the act of adultery

---

7. John Wesley Hanson Jr., *Etiquette of To-day: The Customs and Usages Required by Polite Society* (Robert O. Law, 1896).

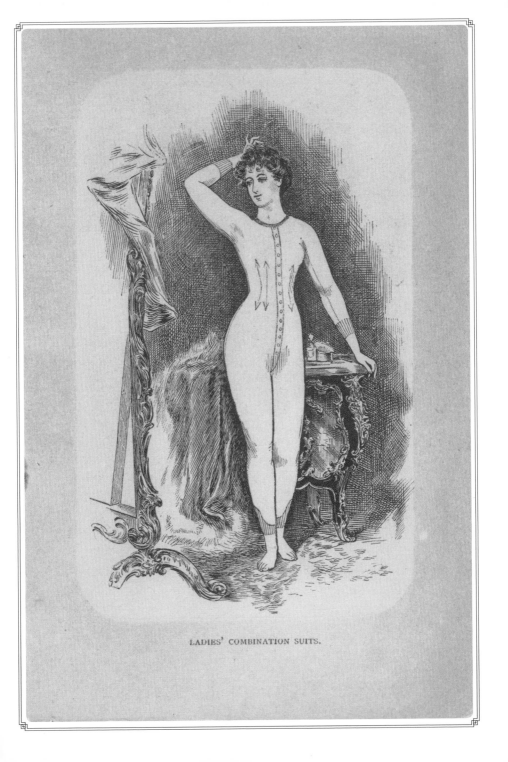

LADIES' COMBINATION SUITS.

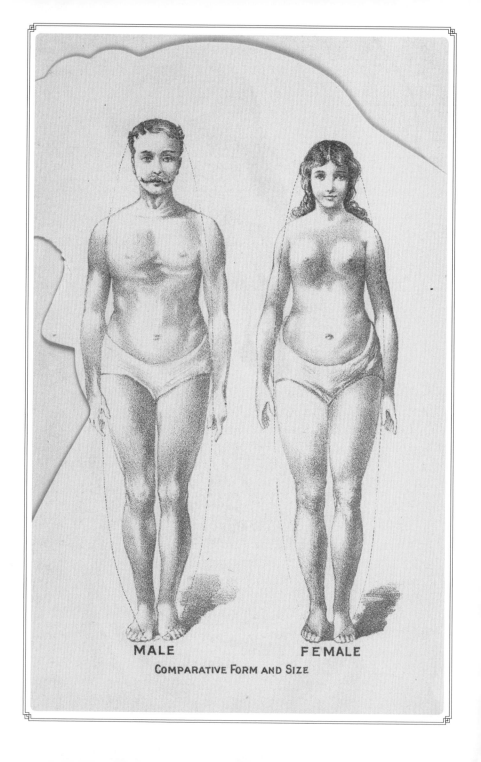

MALE   FEMALE

COMPARATIVE FORM AND SIZE

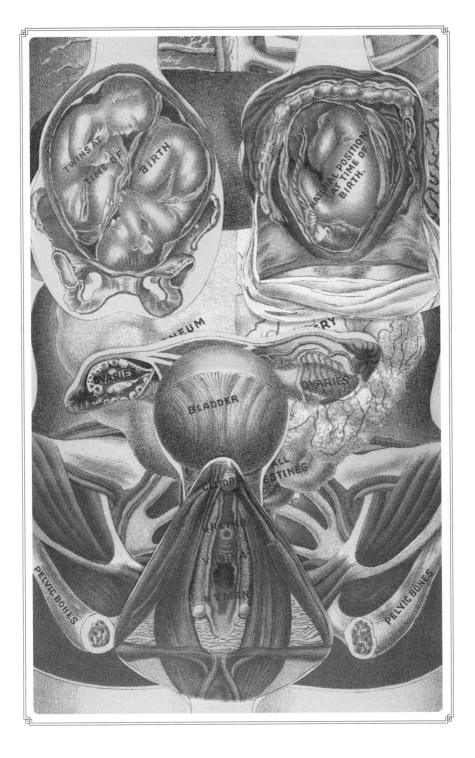

in the guise of "protecting" their wives from their vile (but ultimately human) impulses.

We condemn prostitutes as tarnished, soiled women. The basic service they provide to cure the "devil's impulse" has cost them the respect and protection of society. They are simply trying to make a living in tough times—few other vocations will accept them. The distinction is clear between the upstanding woman and the "fallen" one, who has been (or allowed herself to be) seduced into a life of vice.

Victorian women have their place, and custom and culture keeps them in it. Female-led political reform is greatly frowned upon, even punished. During the Civil War, General Benjamin Butler introduced Order Number 28, in response to society ladies flashing their genitalia at Union soldiers as an act of defiance and revolt. His decree implied that they would be treated as public ladies, available for sale, if they displayed their goods, whatever their intention.

Guidelines for men and homosexual practice are slightly less rigid. Though California enacted an 1850 law condemning sodomy as a crime against nature, in keeping with other states' statutes, laws later in the century have altered the regulation of sexual behavior. In the recent 1897 case, *People v. Boyle,* the court decided that fellatio does not constitute such a punishable sin. The public's moral crusaders prefer not to address matters of male-male love, though it is a widespread practice. Unlike their female compatriots in prostitution, male hustlers meet on street corners or in shaded parks. Demand is high though locale is found wanting. A properly run and truly discreet homosexual brothel stands to give even the most successful madams a run for their money.

The Alameda street cribs and an inmate, 1898. The girls sat in their
windows for blocks, and passengers arriving on the Southern Pacific trains
looking out their windows as they rode down Alameda street to the Arcade
depot saw these scenes.

CHAPTER SEVEN

JACK

I'm a mac. Finest one there is east or west of Alameda.
Was written in the stars on the eve I was born.

Lost my mama that day. Died trying to squeeze me out her
quim. She had syphilis before her lying-in. They told her she
wouldn't last long if she kept me, but Mama insisted. Said she
knew I was her destiny. There was a big full moon that November night, the sky all lit up and twinkling. Deaf Blanche swears
she saw a shooting star pass. And she don't ever lie.

She took me in with her son, George, right from that night and
raised me like I was her own. George is a couple years older than
me, but he was always real slow—Deaf Blanche'd get so mad at
him, damn. He just moved at his own pace, is all. Around that
time she was going with the crib cook Jean Gentil—they were
collecting rent for Ballerino on our crib block. Jean charged

the customers two bits for a hot meal after they'd lain with the girls.

We lived in "little Paree" in the Alameda Street cribs, No. 307. Deaf Blanche had one of the bigger cribs, 'cause she was in tight with Ballerino. He was our landlord, but we didn't see him much. She always went to some fancy-man spot west of the cribs to do the drop.

Me and George were passed around by all the girls on our block when they weren't taking shifts. We slept in back rooms or kept outside when we were old enough. When the railroad workers were on duty, it'd be slow, and the girls would let me play in their bedrooms. I'd sit for hours in front of the cracked glass that hung on the walls in their rooms, admiring myself, making up my face with rouge. Had my own tin my mama left behind.

People have been telling me I was a looker as far back as I remember. "Jack, you're like a little angel," they'd say. Then I'd smile, real slow, slicking my golden hair back with my hands, real casual, so they'd better see my deep blue eyes. "Oh, Jack, those lips of yours, those pillowy lips. . . . You got the devil in that grin."

I was always finding ways to get attention. Back then the only nice things around belonged to the highest-earning girls. I liked to dress up, parading around in their bloomers, with a big black mark on my cheek like they'd draw with soot, just to make them laugh. They practically pissed their drawers when I'd be dancing around the room, make 'em forget all their troubles. No one ever called me a fairy, even when I should've outgrown those games. They'd seen it all anyways.

I understood that most people thought fucking was only meant to be between men and ladies, but I knew it took all kinds. Sure, I acted real normal around them polite folk, talking 'bout manly things, but I never did think there was anything to be ashamed of. It was all making love. With girls, with boys, with men. Whatever combination you wanted, long as you had coin.

Back in those days I'd charge pennies for doin' chores around the cribs. For a dollar I'd sweep the floors, hang the laundry, and plait the girls' hair before bed. Then I started working with the customers out front when I was seven, keeping them in line, offering beer we'd run over from the Basket Saloon down at the Alley.

It wasn't long before I was helping the girls with operations, getting customers in and out on time—Deaf Blanche always said good time management meant more bankroll—and I could count real fast too. It was just easier if I collected the money. I had the brains for it, and it wasn't all that hard. I didn't even need to learn from no one; I just watched their mistakes.

I'd sit on my wooden stool outside of No. 307, chewing tobacco, waiting on the johns to finish, dreaming 'bout the future. My own crib joint, with separate rooms for every girl, and I'd have the whole top floor—weren't any top floors on our block. Just

Right alongside Chinatown, on Alameda and side streets
were the "cribs" of the "Red Light" district. They lined
both sides of Alameda street from about Macy street to
Fifth street, good bad and indifferent houses and dwellings.
About 1898.

rows of rickety wood-frame rooms all crammed up next to one
another. A person could hardly breathe without sneezing on a
neighbor it was so tight.

Naturally I was boss to the other crib bastards. They'd run sup-
plies for a brass check and feel real proud to be earning. Called

me King. George was bigger than all of us, so he'd act tough when there was trouble—there were times when men got out of hand with the girls, coming in loaded on cheap whiskey and forgetting the rules. He's like my brother, George, even if he is a little backward in the head. I try to stay patient with him even if it's hard sometimes.

When I was nine, Deaf Blanche decided I needed proper education like spelling and real arithmetic. I told her I was already plenty educated, but she said my mama would want it, so I went. She sent me over to the Children's Orphan Asylum just a stone's throw from the Alameda Street cribs—up at the corner of Los Angeles and Macy. Those Sisters of Mercy never knew the trouble they were asking for when they took me in.

Nothing but another bunch of bastards at the orphan asylum, but these vics had no idea about the streets, what'd be waiting for them when they were too old for the Sisters to house them. I took it as my duty to educate a group of them boys personally. Even if they weren't wised up like the kids back at the cribs, they were all eager to learn. Had me a nice little crew, some of 'em were fairies too, but mostly 'cause they were too young to know what to do with cunny. I'd already tried it back at the cribs—the girls said it was better I learn how to screw from them than out on the streets. I liked it okay, never did mind who I laid with, as long as someone was paying for my time. I flirted with girls and they flirted back, and sometimes, if they were cute, I'd lie with them. But if I had my choice, it was always with a boy.

I had one real good friend in the asylum, a girl called Frances who was a few years younger. I still go back to visit her. She could read and write really good and taught me lots of fancy words like *elocution* and *vociferous*. Comes in handy to pull them out when people think I'm an oaf 'cause of the way I talk. We used to hide out in the dusty old attic and go through a Webster's I pinched from the Sisters, learning a word a day.

Frances has the soul of an old lady, like she's lived a hundred lifetimes already. Sometimes she scares me how smart she is. Never felt like I wanted to protect someone the way I do with her. The Sisters didn't have a lot of patience for her big words; they were always getting mad at her for something or other. But me? Hell, they couldn't help but like me. Just a wink and a beam and they'd be eating out of my hands.

I used to sneak back home when I could to visit George and the girls. Around that time we all used to go to the swimming hole. Ballerino put it in on the property way back before I was born— summer of '61—and charged ten cents to cool off from the heat. Always thinking of new ways to profit, Ballerino was. He'd let us crib kids in for free; raising the price to twenty-five cents for older gentlemen to watch us swim.

Course I was the main attraction at that hole for the fairy parade—I wore my swimming costume real tight for effect, my hair slicked back with pomade. Made onlookers draw a sharp breath and watch me anxiously. I liked their stares. Meant coins in my pocket. More if I let 'em see my member. I ain't bragging, but I got a nice long pink prick. Had hair since I was seven and been screwing since I was nine. I'd charge 'em a dollar twenty-five if they wanted a mouthful. Usually, though, they'd just masturbate while I watched. That'd cost extra for my time. I kept a notebook in my back pocket to keep track of it all.

Railway car
9th and Santa Fe
1898

1894 Central Park, Los Angeles

I loved those long summer days, when the sun stayed out as late as I did. Skinny-dipping at twilight, the light dappling erect nipples raised above the surface as buoys. Racing a backstroke in tandem with George.

I'd exit the pool performing for my audience, shaking the drops from my hair real slow for them to appreciate. Knowing they were thirsty for the drips of water behind my knees and along my inner elbow, where the skin is pale and supple to suck. I like to be prized.

Back then I was only making change—fine enough for kiddie

games—but by the time I was fourteen, I was planning a more lucrative trade. If I was ever gonna be king of my own castle, I'd have to be right there in the center of the action. I'd been cooped up like an inmate long enough.

As soon as I was out those asylum gates, I got a job as a messenger boy working for Nicolas Oswald. He owns the Belmont crib. He's twenty-nine and getting long in the tooth—but Ballerino likes to keep him around the cribs to manage his ambitions.

I was never gonna settle for the crib life, not me. Always had a taste for improving my station, wanting more. The first money I made I spent on a pair of polished black-heeled boots, real shiny, like the ones that Jean Rappert wore. He was the biggest mac around those parts then—kept thirty-two girls in line at the cribs. I made sure those boots of mine were always real clean. I could catch my reflection in them if the sun was bright. Got a weakness for clothes, the finer stuff. Guess you could call me a dude.

Now I rule my trade over at Central Park, about as far west from the cribs as I can be. Placed right next to the fancy Bunker Hill mansions. My territory runs the whole span of the park—from Olive Street to Hill Street, bordered on the north and south by Fifth and Sixth Streets.

I hardly need to work myself anymore—got a whole network of sporty boys to sell to gentlemen poofs. And a nice secure spot to work from—overgrown with fruit trees and flowering bushes, providing plenty of shade and privacy.

Six in the evening is about our busiest time. Right when they're getting off work, before they have to be home for supper. When the sky's a deep shade of blue and the streetlights are lighting up around the perimeter. I lean back against my regular tree—a cypress—and watch all the up-and-coming members of Los Angeles society taking their dusk promenades through the park to size up my crop. The headquarters of the new Los Angeles Athletic Club is just within spitting distance at Spring between Fourth and Fifth Streets.

I got my boys advertising with a real delicate sign language so I know when to intervene. Sucking on the thumb means potential interest; a lit match's a done deal, and a discarded one signals the sale's off. Conversation carries easily over here, something about the way the wind blows—and I listen closely to the older fairies as they parade around my stable of boys, calculating in my head how much they'll spend.

"Look at all these little chickens—
quite ripe for the plucking, aren't they?"

"So firm their flesh."

"I fancy that one over there—
the golden-haired goose under that tree."

"Mmmmm. He's working his assets in all the right directions. I
can barely choose."

"You're just trying to decide which shelf in the glass menagerie
you're going to display them on."

"Perhaps . . . but I don't want mashers for my bedroom,
I just want them to fluctuate elegantly around me."

"Oh, I do like you—we can have such improper talk together."

———

The johns ask the one they want to lay with for the time, for
a light—they know the score. Got to have certain procedures
in place, you know—otherwise it'd be chaos. I pride myself on
having an assortment of boys to suit every craving. Antagonistic
boxer; gawky bookworm; polished lothario; a long-haired, lean
poet with a broken nose. My boys are all professional; the only
one I ever have trouble with is the Boxer, he's got a nervous dis-
position. Not like the Poet.

The Poet.

Watching him now, all skinnylike—knobbed knees and awk-
ward limbs made even more pronounced by outgrown pants
and shirtsleeves. Big ears that stick out, pale blond hair slicked
back, a lock hanging over one eye. Soft pink earlobes . . .

Third home of the Los Angeles Athletic Club
1889

I could spend hours daydreaming about those earlobes. Him lying on our rumpled bedsheets just a few hours earlier, the lingering trace of his fingers, the bruises around my neck still purple, tingling with anticipation of his red-haired peach-fuzz belly pressed against my own.

Sure has a way about him, the Poet. Always writing in that little pad of his—I took a page when he wasn't looking and keep it crumpled in my pocket:

barefoot in the sand, the only yellow stone in a sea of gray,
thinking about you makes my eyes water.

I ain't the only one with a taste for poetry, as this fella is making a beeline right for him, heading off behind a row of bushes after giving me the signal. I can see them now if I squint my eyes real tight. Nothing to do but wait. I light my sixth smoke of the hour. Oh, I keep to a strict clock—time is money—and I got a brand-new pocket watch—twenty-four-karat gold—with my name engraved right on the back in cursive: *JACK*. Was a gift from a regular—I got me a few who set me up real nice—I have my rent paid for the rest of the year already on a one bedroom above the Basket Saloon by one of them. Got the Poet staying with me now. I make him work Thursday evenings when my regular visits. Another of them loves books. He's always giving me fancy leather-bound ones he gets sent from Europe. That's how I got to reading Oscar Wilde and that French book, *Against Nature*. Says he's trying to better my education. All them fancy folk think you only get learned from books, but I never read one that knew half the things I've seen. Anyway, like I said, I hardly do much trade myself in the park anymore. Only if I'm real bored. I just come here to keep an eye on my business.

I take a long drag of tobacco, exhaling nice and slow as the bushes start to shake. Grunting sounds. I tap my foot impatiently. Never had much patience. The Sisters were always telling me that it was a virtue, but I don't see how virtue gets you anywhere but poor. Finally the bushes stop moving and I see the john emerge, wiping his mouth with a pocket kerchief.

The Poet comes around the bushes, buttoning up his pants and smiling at me. His smile fades as he approaches.

"Got my money?"

I know it's cruel, me being short with him, but I don't like mixing business with pleasure much. He practically throws the coins at me.

"I don't know why you bother to wait. It always makes you sore."

"You should go home."

"You comin'?"

"No. Gotta go to the cribs. See Deaf Blanche. Might take a while."

"I see."

I look at my watch again, see the seconds tick by.

"Jack? You been gone the last five nights, I thought we could stay in together . . . at least till the midnight shift."

Shit. Got no time for emotional scenes with anyone, that's why I never stay too long; they start asking questions—where you going, where you been, who you been with?

"Don't wait up."

I watch him walk away. Real slow like he's hoping I'll call out to him, tell him to come back. But I got things to do, and I don't need anyone slowing my roll.

I was just gonna shut my eyes a minute, wait for him to round the corner and disappear. But what's that rustling of leaves and the faintest sound of footsteps? He's come back, interrupting me when I'm busy?

I open my eyes real slow, narrowing them into darts.

There in the shadows a figure is watching me—appeared just like vapor or a vampire. Starts walking toward me. Elegantly dressed, a well-cut cape with a hood pulled down low over pale skin. The scent of rose oil mixed with musk. A woman. She looked familiar, but I was sure I'd never seen her before.

She extended a hand to me by way of introduction, and in an English accent, she said, "I am Cora Phillips."

I'd heard of her, she runs that fancy Golden Lion house over on Alameda. Down at the cribs, Deaf Blanche was talking about her—all the high-priced madams in town had their drawers in a bundle over Cora. They said no one except her preferred clients and staff knew what she looked like. Pearl Morton let word out that she'd pay handsomely for any information, so this was sure to fetch a good price.

"I come to you with a proposal."

"Normally don't service your kind, ma'am; but for an extra fee—"

"It isn't your skill in the bedroom I require." She searched my face.

I nodded at her to continue.

"How would you like to take over my operation?"

"Ha!"

The woman was either loaded or nutty. Who had ever heard of a male madam?

"I am quite serious. I would train you myself—you would take over the house, the stable—all at your disposal."

"This a con?"

"No, of course not."

"So what's the hitch?"

She paused, taking a sharp breath.

"I have a very particular private backer who would have final approval over your appointment."

"But why do you want to get out of the business, lady? From what I hear you're making a fortune in gold bricks over there."

"I want out, that is all you need to know. I have had eyes on you, so I know you are capable of discretion. I am certain he would be pleased. . . ."

"He?"

"You will meet him soon enough if you accept."

"I'll have to think it over."

Cora fingered the tassels of her cloak, tucking a loose lock of hair back under her hood.

"I must take my leave. Come to my house at dawn, you know where it is. Go around the back to the small door off the alley and ring the bell. My butler Emerson will show you to my drawing room. You can wait for me there."

And with that she turned on her heels and headed back into the shadows, leaving me to chew on her proposition.

A house of my own. A full stable of boys. Handpicked clientele. No expense spared. I'd pictured it so many times. Hallways lined in black velvet with gold piping. Six boys on display in a small antechamber with mirrored walls on three sides. Their buck-naked asses on display like those Greek statues—turning around slowly for inspection. A gilt one-way mirror behind which customers could choose for the evening.

Cora hadn't mentioned a change in operations, but she sure seemed desperate to hand over her trade. I'm sure I could persuade her. Why shouldn't the boys have a place to play? It'd be highly profitable, with a double charge to keep the activity secret. All these customers of mine have real nice society wives, you know.

I mean, I'm on the edge of seventeen now, practically over the hill. A man's gotta set his mind to ambition if he's ever gonna make something of himself. I stub out another cigarette, decide to end my shift early; I can't wait to tell the Poet the news.

But I am too late.

From across the darkened street I watch the Poet pace the confines of our small digs above the Basket Saloon. I watch him take inventory one last time. Watch him walk out the door, all his belongings in a small burlap sack over his shoulder. Watch him until he disappears round the bend, toward the railroad tracks.

He left me a note on our unmade bed.

Waking walking sleeping dreaming
I can't concentrate you have me distracted
I fall apart before I start
Lulled only by the rhythm of your sighs
I couldn't hear before I wasn't listening
I don't want to know the truth
it's better this way trust me

Hell, I don't know about all this pain and suffering for love. If it feels good, then I'm all for it, but the moment it turns sour is my cue to be gone. Guess he beat me to it this time. I mean, life's too short to be distracted by tenderness and too long if you're poor. Can't afford any interference if you're ever gonna be a success on this earth.

And what do poets know about love, anyway? What do they read in those fancy books they're always buried in? Books don't know about love. Those ain't real stories. Just some tall tales dreamed up for bored ladies. Love can be bought. Love can be sold. I know just about everything there is to know about love. Known it all since I came into this world. Was written right there in the stars.

CHAPTER EIGHT

YOUTH

I remember it was unseasonably cold that day. The first time I saw you. I wore my new overcoat from City of Paris, double-breasted with big horn buttons. I bought the evening edition of the Herald from the boy in the lobby and had it tucked under my arm. I planned to sit in the park and read before supper.

But as I walked the paths toward the row of benches, there you were, leaning casually against a cypress tree, and I found I couldn't sit at all. The collar of your shirt turned up for protection against the crisp air. Your hands shoved in your pockets when they weren't lighting another cigarette. Waiting.

I must have walked around in circles for an hour, summoning my courage to approach.

I shut out the calls of the others, hungry for the notes burning holes in my pocket, even the beautiful redheaded one a little older than you. Told me he was a descendant of a musketeer. I looked down at my paper, scanning the ink, until he walked away.

Then I closed my eyes, thinking of the bulge in your pants straining against fabric, my lips around your member, thrusting yourself deeper into my mouth, hallucinatory undulations taking me over.

Under my coat my trousers rose. I folded the paper across my lap, peering around to see if you were watching. Feeling disappointed—you'd left your post.

I came every night that week, the same routine, late for supper several times. All the while thinking of you, wishing your hands would brush against mine. Walking the paths distracted by the colors of the leaves, wondering if they were more real than we would ever be—silly daydreams that hadn't occurred since I was a boy.

And every time I crossed your path, slowing my pace to a crawl, hoping you'd look at me, clearing my throat to utter a greeting, I would waver once more.

It was the following Tuesday that you finally glanced up as I rounded the bend, cracking your mouth into a wide smile. It took a while to appreciate your grin was meant for me, hidden as it was behind veils of smoke rising up. Licking the tobacco stuck to your bottom lip, breath hot and sweet. I could barely breathe myself as I moved toward you, anticipating rejection, bracing myself for the heartbreak of your lips.

Without a word, you turned and walked toward a line of hedges behind the gazebo. I followed, obedient, stopping only when you did, tucked safely inside the shade of the shrubbery. You held out your hand, and I fumbled in my trousers, my fingers shaking, pulling out a wad of notes and pressing them into your palm.

Silently, you took me, and a jolt went through my bones like I'd never recover. Your tongue on my neck, turning me over and pushing me into the branches, a mouthful of foliage tasting like your sweat as you pounded me into submission. Your fluids dripping down my legs. Wanting it all over again as soon as you had your way.

I go home, smelling of us, masking our tryst in heavy cologne. She's already asleep, the children tucked away safely. I creep in, murmuring your name as I crawl into the sheets besides her, turning my back so I can smile in the dark. Counting the hours, counting my change, until I can see you again.

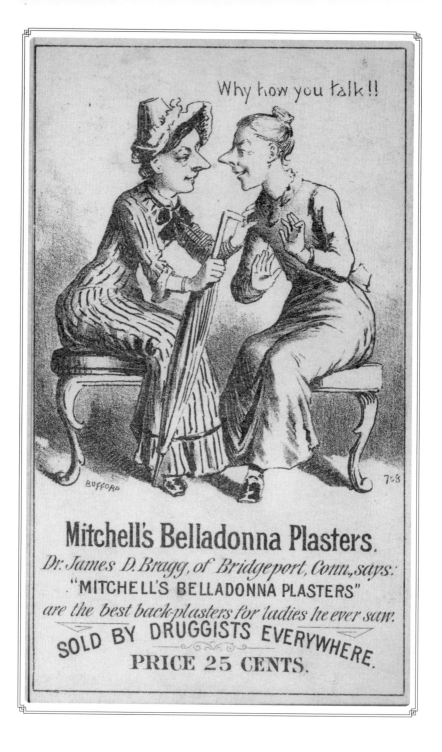

CHAPTER NINE

COSMETICS

Several centuries ago, cosmetics were the province of actresses and prostitutes, also known as painted ladies. It was said that ". . . a painted face is enough to destroy the Reputation of her that uses it."[8] Now, in 1897, the use of cosmetics and face paint has spread well beyond the narrow confines of social strata or geography. Yet the feminine ideal for upstanding moral ladies

---

8. From *The Ladies Dictionary,* a 1694 English etiquette and beauty bible. The index also offers advice on the following topics: "breasts hanging down or large, how to make them plump and round"; "deformity . . . how ladies ought to bear it with patience"; "hands, how to make them fair and white, with small veins"; "husband, whether lawful for a young lady to pray for one"; "obedient wives"; "occasions of falling in love to be avoided"; "virginity, its wonderful effects"; "virgins of the younger sort"; "wife, advice about choosing a good one."

remains a pale "un-spoilt" complexion, free of paints and arti-
fice. Regardless, it requires great effort to achieve this "natural"
look.

For those women not inherently endowed with fair skin, they
must resort to painting their faces with white powders made
from solutions containing talc, bismuth, oyster shells, and seed
pearls dissolved in acid. To highlight wan complexions, women
artistically draw themselves additional veins with blue grease
pencils or a paste of chalk, gum arabic water, and blue dye.

Druggists sell commercially produced creams to make the skin
radiant; their ingredients often including mercury, arsenic, and
lead. It is well-known that absorbing lead can cause convulsion
of the limbs, if not paralysis and death. Alas, to be beautiful is
to suffer. A "Bloom of Youth" lotion for "whitening" has led to
hundreds of medical ailments. Arsenic is used as a facial wash
and is also available in digestible forms, such as Dr. Campbell's
Safe Arsenic Complexion Wafers. Advertised in *Vogue* and sold
by low-cost retailers and catalogs, these solutions are promoted
as providing clear and brilliant complexions not obtainable
by external applications, as well as being beneficial to general
health.

For women unable to afford such luxury goods but desperate for
the right pallor, they can rub their faces with bread crumbs; eat
chalk, slate, and tea grounds; suck on lead pencils; sip vinegar;
or be bled.

First electric
street lamp
Main Street near
Commercial
1882

Late 19th-century snake-oil
salesman plying his wares

Any threat to a woman's lily-white appearance is cause for alarm. When electric streetlamps were introduced to Los Angeles in 1882, the gas company protested, saying that electric light had a bad effect on ladies' complexions. A recipe in an 1896 issue of the *Los Angeles Evening Herald* suggested that women bathe their face two to three times a day with buttermilk and wear a thin gauze veil for protection against the sun. Even excessive exposure to moonlight is warned against, for its supposedly harsh effects on uncovered skin.

Although many Victorian women wear rouge sparingly, few advertise the fact. A light, rosy glow suggesting the bloom of youth is acceptable. The prostitute's toilette is as elaborate as the stage actress preparing to stand out under harsh theatrical lights. Fallen women are known to over-rouge their bad complexions. They disguise their profession by using skin-whitening powder on their face and wearing pale kid gloves over callused hands. The reddish tone of their wrists gives them away.

Recipes for makeup are passed along by word of mouth and via the polite pages of *Godey's Lady Books*. A kitchen cosmetic recipe for "pearl water" includes rosemary, spritzs of wine, and the best Spanish oil soap—meant to be excellent at removing freckles.[9] "Pearl" powder whitens the skin and blackened cork darkens eyebrows and lashes. Home remedies include rouge

---

9. Godey's Lady Book, 1855.

papers to give the cheeks a flushed glow; blush is also painted just under the eyelids to make the eyes more prominent.

Eyelashes can be oiled to create a dewy look and drops of belladonna, a poisonous herb, used to enlarge the pupils. Fashionable ladies bathe their eyes in prussic acid to enhance their whiteness and brilliancy. A variety of balsams for the eyes are available over the counter, but in a pinch, it is suggested that eating a sugar cube soaked in rubbing alcohol or cologne just before going to a party would brighten the eyes.

Pharmacies and snake-oil salesmen sell countless tinctures to correct faults in one's features. After all, "if women are to govern, control, manage, influence, and retain the adoration of husbands, fathers, brothers, lovers, or even cousins, they must look their prettiest at all times."[10] Good lighting helps to mask imperfections. The finer houses wisely choose candlelight chandeliers in boudoirs and dimmed electric lighting in parlor rooms; crib joints make do with single gas lanterns.

---

10. Hanson, *Etiquette of To-Day*.

Los Angeles Orphan Asylum.

Conducted by "The Sisters" - Catholic.

- In Course -

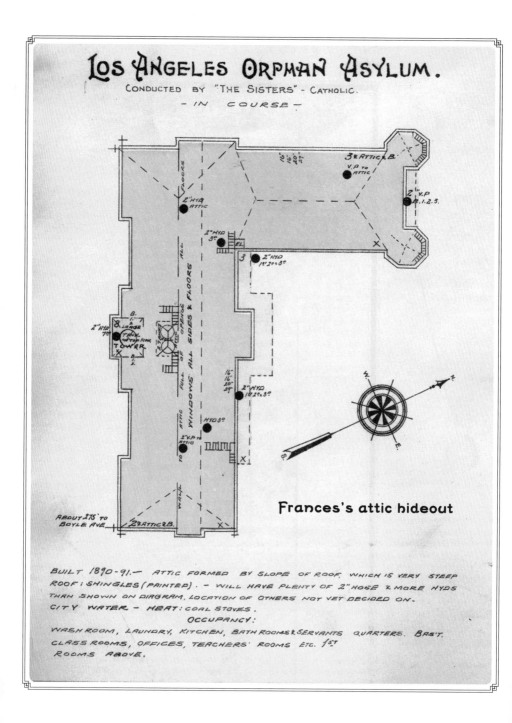

Frances's attic hideout

Built 1890-91. — Attic formed by slope of roof, which is very steep
Roof: Shingles (painted). — Will have plenty of 2" hose & more hyds
than shown on diagram. Location of others not yet decided on. —
City Water — Heat: Coal Stoves.

Occupancy:

Wash room, Laundry, Kitchen, Bath rooms & Servants quarters. Bas't.
Class rooms, Offices, Teachers' rooms etc. 1st
Rooms above.

CHAPTER TEN

FRANCES

The attic is the only place I can be alone. Think. Usually it's so noisy I can't even hear my own breath. I come up here a lot to sit under the wooden rafters, just daydreaming. I made all the watercolors lining the dusty windowsills—just little things I like, butterflies and ladybugs. They make the room a little cheerier. I have a little paint set and a horsehair brush—the colors are almost worn down and most of the brush hairs have broken off. But I don't care. I'm happiest by myself watercoloring with no one disturbing me.

I live in the Children's Orphan Asylum, a big brick building at the corner of Alameda and Macy Streets, along with my three hundred fellow inmates, all of us imprisoned as wards of the state—at least until we're turned out to the streets on our fourteenth birthdays. When we are adults. Only half of us

HAN ASYLUM   : CURLETT · EISEN · & · CUTBERTSON :
                    · · ARCHITECTS · ·

sleep here; the rest leave before supper, to earn their keep at home.

Mother Superior Cecilia runs the asylum. I don't much like her, and she doesn't much like me. The other Sisters are okay. Sister Margaret is my favorite, at least she's kind. Mother Superior Cecilia doesn't have patience for kindness.

On the communal girls' floor, we lie in orderly rows and fall asleep after reciting evening prayers.

> *Now I lay me down to sleep,*
> *I pray the Lord my soul to keep,*
> *If I shall die before I wake,*
> *I pray the Lord my soul to take. Amen.*

But I've always had trouble sleeping. I get so restless, lying there with everyone else in the dark. So I steal up here, two floors above where everyone else is slumbering.

Not much in here to speak of 'cept for a large glass mirror in the corner, clouded with smudges and dirt. I don't even know how it even got up here—we're not supposed to be vain and look at ourselves. Mother Superior Cecilia would have a fit if she knew about it. Maybe some Sister left it long ago. The attic is the only room in the whole building without iron bars on the windows. From here I can see straight across Alameda Street, almost to the buildings on Main Street if the sky is clear. It's always drafty up here—in the whole building, really—and I dream of warm fires and roast meats while I look at the stars. Counting. Making wishes.

Most nights I watch the man who lives next door. I stare at him as he paces back and forth, his shadow disappearing and reappearing between the windows of his stone estate. I can look out right over the top of the iron gates that border the asylum into his overgrown garden next door. Statues litter his lawn, some overturned onto their sides like stone figures inhabiting an ancient ghostly battlefield. Tangles of ivy conceal the untended edges of his grounds, their leaves extending across the lawn, partly covering a small lily pond. He keeps a light glowing in his library window, and I can just make out his silhouette now, slumped in a chair. I wonder what keeps him awake.

Sometimes I consider slipping out, beyond the iron gates skirting the grounds, and going all the way to the edge of his window, just to see him up close. I even dream that he might invite me in, give me a hot drink and something to eat. But we aren't allowed off the grounds except under the Sisters' supervision. Incoming visitors must be on official business. Rarely, on special occasions, so special the newspaper sends a man to the asylum to meet with Mother Superior Cecilia and prints the story, we get to leave. They can't say no when it's official. Next week we're going to the circus. I'm going to wear my hair in the new French plaits that my best friend Molly taught me.

Baron Littlefinger with Minnie Warren and his brother, Count Rosebud.

1899

NOTICE:

May 24, 1897

The *Los Angeles Times* extends an invitation to all newsboys and inmates of all orphan asylums and other juvenile charitable institutions to a special performance at 10 o'clock Tuesday morning.

Appearing in person will be Los Angeles's own Baron Littlefinger and brother, Count Rosebud.

Practically every day here is pretty much the same: morning prayers, breakfast, elocution, arithmetic, supper, history lessons, and vespers. Bells signal each hour and schedules written in ink are tacked to the walls of our quarters so we won't be late. Mealtimes are the worst. Mushy, lumpy, sloppy bowls of gruel—the cook doesn't use any seasoning—and you have to eat it all, every last drop, or you get your knuckles rapped with the wooden rulers the Sisters carry.

The weekends are the hardest. The hours until Monday feel endless. Tuesdays and Fridays we have history and music lessons. Those are my favorite days. We have a music room on the first floor with a grand piano in it. Our music teacher, Monsieur Legasse, donated it himself. He's French. He came here to recover from consumption, but he's still frail and coughs a lot. The other girls are scared of his sickness, but I don't mind it. He doesn't have any children of his own, so he has a lot of time to spend with us.

I like history lessons too. I love to imagine what life was like in other places and times, how things came to be. Sometimes when Sister Margaret shows picture books, I have the strangest feeling that I've been there before, seen those things myself.

But that's impossible, of course. The only memories I have are the ones made here at the asylum. I've no idea at all where I was actually born. I've been here since I was just an infant wrapped up in swaddling cloth. This has been my home for thirteen and a half years now. Most of the other inmates in my dormitory

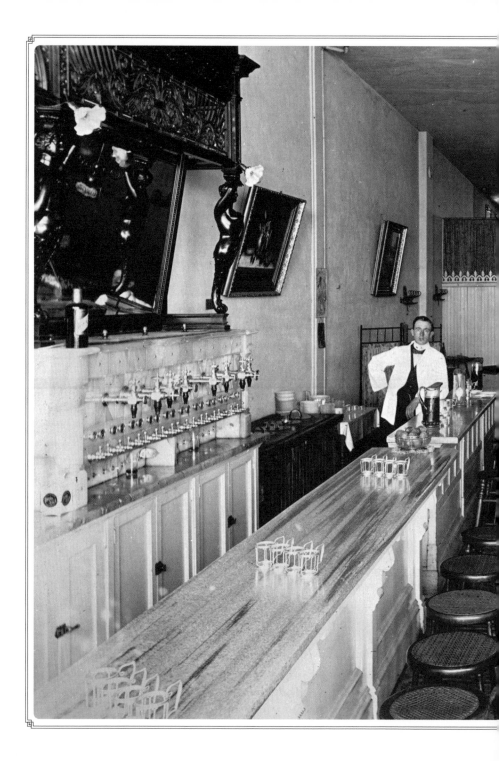

Wells Candy Store
1897

came when I did. But that doesn't mean we share confidences. The other girls think I'm strange 'cause I like to keep to myself, reading books and dreaming. I'm mostly okay on my own, but sometimes I get lonely, wish I had someone to count the stars with. Molly is my only friend in here besides Jack, but he's gone now. He's seventeen, so he left a few years back, but he still comes to visit me. Used to take care of me when he was in here—no one would tease me 'cause they were all afraid of him.

Molly's not a boarder, though, like Jack and me—she's a scullery maid who is a few years older than me, been getting her monthlies for a while now. Has to use those suspender belts with the linen pads and starch them clean after. I haven't gotten mine yet.

Molly and Jack were both born down the block in the Alameda Street cribs. They've known each other since they were little. Molly and Jack talk about the cribs like it's a place to leave, but it sounded nice to me. They said it was a hard life, doing "women's work." I think it has something to do with your monthlies and being ready to be a woman. Entertaining. Earning a living. I don't understand it exactly, but whenever Molly tried to explain it, Jack shut her up good.

Anyway, if it wasn't for Molly and Jack I wouldn't know about the real world at all. What Los Angeles is like. I love hearing Molly talk about the milliners' shops with their rows of colored ostrich feathers, the new cable cars. I even like to hear her grocer's lists—I can just picture rows of oranges and lemons all shiny and tart.

The other inmates are content to be the cutest little bastards in the orphanage, vying for Mother Superior Cecilia's attention. But not me. I want something more. Not exactly sure what yet, but someplace else, someone else to belong to.

All that's left behind to connect us with the parents who gave us up are single tokens. Mother Superior Cecilia keeps them locked in her desk, but Molly lifted her key from the master key ring, and one night I unlocked it while she stood guard. Inside I found:

a single gold key

a pear-shaped, yellow glass pendant

a smashed thimble

a loose button

a thin carved ivory fish

a tiny ring with a red stone in the center and a little lock
   and key attached to its sides

a silver tag with rubbed-off writing

a heart-shaped locket with the words "You have my heart
   though we must part, I.W., Sept. 6, 1856"

a tiny green knit bag with the initials M.D. embroidered in
   mustard yellow

a tin container of rouge

a metal bracelet with a large lock attached

a ribbon with a tiny cameo woven into the threads

a mother-of-pearl pendant with the initials E.L.

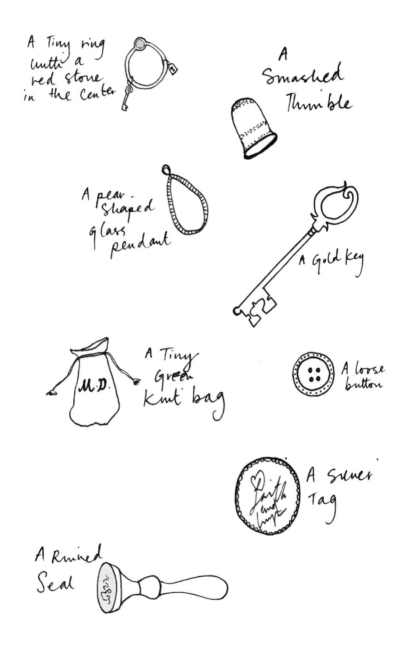

A Tiny ring with a red stone in the Center

A Smashed Thimble

A pear-shaped glass pendant

A Gold key

A Tiny Green knit bag

M.D.

A loose button

A Silver Tag

A Ruined Seal

A Beaded
Bracelet
with a
Charm

A metal bracelet
with a Lock

A Tiny Carved
Ivory fish

A Rusted
Lock

A Tin Container
of Rouge

A mother of
pearl pendant

E.L.

You HAVE MY
HEART, THOU
WE MUST
PART, I.W.
SEPT. 6,
1856

A Heart-shaped
locket

A Ribbon with
a tiny Cameo woven
into its threads

a beaded bracelet with a charm
a ruined seal, indecipherable
a rusted lock
a pendant in the shape of a small fist

I knew none of these belonged to me. Disappointed, I pulled the drawer out farther, reaching my arm into its recesses and found a dark leather box, edged in gilt. Inside, nestled in velvet, was a brooch made from a circle of pearls set in gold, surrounding a miniature portrait of an eye. I turned it over and saw the engraving on the back:

Frances

I'd never imagined anything so handsome. I could hardly believe that it might belong to me. But there my name was, right on the back. My mother must have been well-heeled to leave me with such fine jewelry. I'll never know. Of course I had to take it.

Untying the ribbon from my hair, I threaded it through the pin of the brooch. It was hard to do 'cause its clasp was so tarnished. Outside the room, Molly knocked on the door three times, our signal that someone was coming. Pushing with force on the clasp to close it, I pricked my thumb. Blood dripped from my finger.

Three more knocks at the door, followed by another three. Molly began to pound. I placed the box back inside the far reaches of the drawer and locked it shut. I finally closed the brooch on the ribbon and tied it around my neck, tucking it underneath my pinafore. On my apron were three tiny spots of blood. Mother Superior Cecilia would be angry. She always singled me out for a lecture.

I tiptoed down a set of creaky stairs and quietly slipped into my dormitory, taking my place next to the other kneeling girls, their hands folded in prayer. Mother Superior Cecilia raised her eyebrows at my late entry.

"Late again, Frances? That'll be one week of morning laundry duty for you."

"Yes, Mother Superior."

"And is that a smudge on your nightdress?"

I look down at the bloodstains on my crisp linen.

"What do we say, children?"

"Cleanliness is next to Godliness, Mother Superior."

"That's right, children. Dirt is the Devil's tool. God doesn't love those who attract filth." Mother Superior Cecilia looked at me pointedly.

"Two weeks of morning laundry then, Frances, till you learn your lesson."

I nod my head. Six more months till I don't have to hear about

Orphan children
on an outing
circa 1905

God and dirt and the Devil. I don't believe in any of it, anyway. They say if we're real good and listen hard God will talk to us, but I've never heard him. If God is supposed to love us so much, why did he leave me here?

"All right, children. Lights out."

Mother Superior Cecilia turned on her heels to leave, shutting the lights off. The other girls scrambled into bed, shooting resentful looks at me. Ruth narrowed her eyes, preparing to reprimand me in front of the others. She's already fourteen, but the Sisters are letting her stay on another few months to lead us by her good example.

"Always acting so high–and-mighty, thinking she can come and go as she pleases, and no care to keep herself clean."

"Shut up, Ruth."

The other girls gasped at my curse. No one dares challenge Ruth. It's an unspoken rule that she's in charge of our dormitory. But I don't follow anyone, especially her.

"Mind yourself, Frances. You wouldn't want Mother Superior finding out where you get to every night now, would you?"

"Just you try . . ."

"Jack ain't here to protect you no more, Frances. Better watch how you speak."

The door to the dormitory opened and Mother Superior Cecilia poked her head back in.

"I should not be hearing any noise after lights out or it's an extra hour of vespers for you all."

We fell silent as the door closed. Ruth and I locked eyes in the darkened room, neither of us speaking. Finally, Ruth looked away, grunting.

That Ruth doesn't even know what she's talking about. Jack showed me all the private corridors and crannies in this place. No one has ever found out where I go to, after lights out. The attic is my shelter.

"Miss Frances! Miss Frances!"

The sound of Molly's voice calling to me from the other end of the attic startles me. She's standing in front of the mirror admiring herself. She's the only one who comes up here, besides me. Mostly to look at the glass and fix her hair before her shift ends.

"Stop your daydreamin'. Come over here and help me pin my hair. Want to do it like one of them Gibson Girls in the magazines. Got to look nice tonight—meetin' Anna and Bernadette later for dancin'."

"I wish I could go dancing."

"You'll be dancin' the cakewalk soon enough, Miss Frances. Now quit starin' out that window and git over here!"

I join reluctantly, considering my own reflection alongside hers.

Dismal brown eyes stare back at me, partially covered by over-grown bangs. Brunette hair, straight and mousy, hangs down to the middle of my back, held in place with a blue grosgrain ribbon Molly gave me for my last birthday. On my feet a pair of well-worn boots with knotted laces come up above my ankles. My dress, modest, gray—once cream—ends just below my knees. I made it myself in the dressmaking rooms on the second floor of the asylum. The Sisters teach us useful skills—idle hands are the Devil's tool and all.

All in all, I wasn't much to look at. I let out a long sigh. "I wish I weren't so plain."

"Ah, c'mon now, Miss Frances, you're not seein' clear. We can gussie you right up."

I shrug my shoulders and let her take charge, wincing as she brushes my hair with her coarse-bristle brush, pinching my cheeks to bring a flush.

"That's better, Miss Frances. Oooh, if we had some coin we could fix you just like one of them ladies from Pearl Morton's house—I saw them today at Nadeau's General on Spring Street—they wear satin ribbons in their hair, Miss Frances . . .

Oh! And embroidered shawls round their shoulders. And I saw one lady with oxblood boots, it's true!"

"Oh! I'd love to have oxblood boots of my own! I wish I could live there."

"How much more time you got—six months till your birthday?"

I nod my head.

"Well, not long to wait. Pearl's always looking for young blood. We jus' gotta get you seeming proper."

I saw Pearl Morton once. She was talking to Mother Superior Cecilia when I was out by the gated boundary of the lawn in front of the asylum. She was here visiting with the Fat Man, one of the asylum's patrons, on his inspection rounds. We never knew his name, but everyone called him that 'cause of his heft. A dotted black veil hung over Pearl's head all the way to her waist, covering her bright yellow hair. Later, Molly told me that Pearl always wore the veil in public to mask her complexion, supposedly ruined years ago by diphtheria.

Waiting outside in Pearl's carriage was the most beautiful lady I'd ever seen. Even now I can't recall if she came to me in a dream, or, if awake, my path happened upon hers. I have hazy impressions that come flickering in when I close my eyes.

The stiff silk of her outerdress was an unsettling muddy green, as if black ink had spilt in the dye. Her bodice was stitched at her waist in a deep V, a wasp-waisted silhouette above full skirts. Pintucked pleats rose and fell in columns, vertical lines interrupted only by the curves around her breasts.

A bustle at the back of her figure, padded with crinoline and horsehair, stood erect. The cuffs of her sleeves ended in widow's peaks above her wrists, fastened on the underside with a handful of covered buttons. Two patches of forearm revealed their ruddiness before disappearing into pale gray kid gloves that enshrouded her hands. Her slender throat was encircled by a length of velvet ribbon.

I could barely breathe, so intoxicated was I by her brightness and glitter. Ornaments dangling, jangling from every surface. A cacophony of colors—layers of petticoats—marigold, violet, and blue. Her figure curving in and out. Roundness where I had none. Breakable curves. Glassy pupils, hollow under-eyes rimmed with rouge paper and framed above by lashes blackened with cork.

Painted lips.

As I stared at her, transfixed, the wind picked up and I caught her scent—chalk powder, fresh hides, vinegar solution, and bootblack. The aroma of industry entangled in her musk. A delicious smell of possibilities and pleasure, shiny coins jingling

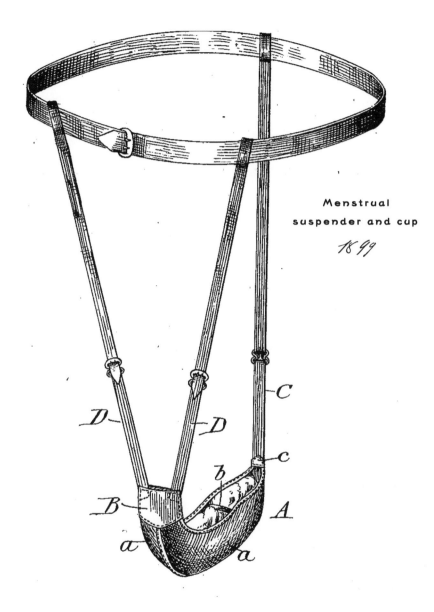

Menstrual
suspender and cup

1899

in silk purses. Her fragrance seeped through me, expanding within my limbs till my insides were filled.

How I wanted to nestle in her crinolines, roll in her silks, lie among her ostrich feathers, entombed, cocooned.

"Miss Frances! Miss Frances! Hello! Where are you off to in that head of yours?"

"Sorry, Molly, I was just . . . tell me again about Pearl's house."

Molly let out a long sigh. "Again? Oh, all right. Feel like I've done told you a hundred times before. Well, it's just beautiful, all red carpeting and polished wood banisters. Real crystal chande-liers in every room and a solid-gold bathtub. Every lady of the house has her own maid. I wouldn't mind being a dressing maid there. Anything's better than this itchy uniform. I heard even the kitchen maids get to wear real stockings!"

"Real stockings?"

"Yes, and satin bows to keep the tops up too."

"You think I could be a lady of the house?"

"Ah, Miss Frances, don't let Jack hear you talk like that. He don't like me encouragin' you. Wants to set you up with somethin' nice and respectable, he does."

"But I don't want to be respectable. I want nice things and a home like Pearl's. I can't wait to be a real woman."

"You sure about that? It ain't gonna be easy work at Pearl's."

"What's so hard about entertaining gentlemen and lounging around in silks? Sounds nice to me."

"Oh, Miss Frances, you got lots to learn. But you got time for that yet. Be learned more than you want soon enough. You haven't even got your monthlies yet and talkin' bout bein' a woman . . ."

I blush bright red. "Molly!"

"I'm sorry, Miss Frances. Sometimes I forget my place. C'mon now, look at yourself in the glass. You do look almost like a woman if you'd just stand up straight and emphasize those rosebuds of yours."

I can hardly feel the tiny bumps growing under my pinafore. But I try to see what she's seeing in the glass. My cheeks are flushed, my eyes bright. The sensation in my stomach—excitement, fear—grows fiercer as each day passes closer to my birthday. Won't be long now before I'm on the outside of these brick walls and iron gates. I can't wait. To really be living. Like Jack is. I bet this city has never even known a woman like I am going to be.

ATTENTION OF PHYSICIANS IS CALLED TO THE

𝕻𝖆𝖈𝖎𝖋𝖎𝖈 𝕳𝖔𝖘𝖕𝖎𝖙𝖆𝖑.

A Private Institution for the especial treatment of

GYNECOLOGICAL AND LYING-IN PATIENTS,

AS WELL AS OTHER OPERATIVE CASES.

This institution was opened in Los Angeles August 1st 1887, since which there has been treated within its walls quite a variety of cases, capital as well as minor, with gratifying success.

The location of the Hospital has been much improved by a change from 121 Winston Street, to 447 South Fort Street, near Sixth Street and on the line of the Los Angeles Cable Railway.

Physicians in distant places, where there are poor conveniences for operations, can send their patients here and feel that all that skill and care can accomplish will be done for them.

Physicians in Los Angeles and vicinity, who place their patients in this 'Institution can attend and operate on them and receive every courtesy.

Charges will be according to room occupied, care required and the treatment or operation necessary.

Address for further particulars either of the undersigned.

Dr. WALTER LINDLEY.

Dr. FRANCIS L. HAYNES.

Dr. J. E. COWLES. *

447 South Fort Street,   Los Angeles, Cal.

* Dr. Cowles late for eighteen months Resident Physician and Surgeon N. Y. Lying-In Hospital is now physician in charge.

CHAPTER ELEVEN

SEXUAL HYGIENE

Prophylactics are required by the madams in the finer houses of prostitution. Multitudes are in use. Parisian prostitutes favor oil and a solution of caustic soda. Civil War soldiers called rubbers (linen treated with antiseptic chemicals or animal intestines softened by lye and sulfur) "French ticklers."

Though twenty-one states passed anti-contraceptive laws in 1879, by 1890 an over-the-counter solution called Darby's Prophylactic Fluid was sold in an aqua glass bottle. By 1895 most brothels preferred a salve of Vaseline and boric acid to the condom.

House doctors visit the better-class brothels every few days to check for disease. Prostitutes in plush bordellos are required to wash customers carefully with soap and water before getting down to business, though not all are vigilant in their efforts. The lower the dive, the less it is likely to have a physician on call.

Public clinics serve street prostitutes, who are diagnosed and examined like specimens for medical reviews.[11]

Vaginal injections of carbolic acid to prevent conception and neutralize venereal disease are common among prostitutes and housewives alike, and there are advertisements for vaginal syringes in broadsheets across America. Other douches include warm/cold water; bicarbonate of soda; borax; mercury; alum; diluted vinegar; lysol; creolin; and lemon juice and whiskey, combined.

Back-alley abortions are the only option for those too late to sterilize the womb after intercourse; to risk bringing the unwanted child of a john into the world renders its mother unfit for her work. For married couples to prevent conception,

---

11. "Age 21. Left ovary and tube removed. 2 children. 2 miscarriages. Gonorrhea.

Age 22. Heroin habit. Pregnant. Probably high-grade feebleminded.

Age 22. Appendix, ovary, and tube removed. Alcoholic. Gonorrhea.

Age 26. Rectal abcess. 1 stillbirth. 2 illegitimate children. Like a fifth-grade girl and capable of slight improvement.

Age 25. Alcohol and cocaine. Very nervous. Gonorrhea. Temperamental and emotional instability.

Age 20. Has had abortion. Gonorrhea.

Age 16. No defects. Syphilis and gonorrhea."

Walter Clarke, "Prostitution and Mental Deficiency," *Social Hygiene*, June 1915.

Postal Regulations—Cont'd.

Packages may have sender's address written on the wrapper and a written list of the articles contained in the package; any letter, number or mark by which it can be identified, but nothing whatever in the way of correspondence or information beyond this. All fourth class matter must be unsealed and wrapped so that it can be readily inspected without injury to the wrapper, and not exceeding four pounds in weight of any one package.

With the single exception of original packets put up by the manufacturers which are sealed by internal revenue stamps, ALL MAIL MATTER NOT SENT AT LETTER RATES MUST BE LEFT OPEN TO INSPECTION BY THE POST OFFICE AUTHORITIES. No articles, other than letters and postal cards, can be returned to the senders on request, unless again fully prepaid; nor can they be advertised; but if found undeliverable or uncalled for, they will be sent to the dead letter office. Mail matter of the third and fourth class is not assorted and put up with, or in the same manner as letters, being placed loose in canvas sacks and not

in locked pouches; and, of course, whenever it is necessary, on account of unusual accumulation of mail matter or for other reasons, to give preference in dispatch, it is always accorded to first class matter.

Unmailable Matter.—Liquids, poisons, explosive and inflammable articles, fatty substance easily liquefiable, live or dead animals (not stuffed), live insects and reptiles, fruits or vegetable matter liable to decomposition, comb honey, pastes or confections, guano, and other substances exhaling a bad odor, are regarded as in themselves, either from their form or nature, within the inhibitions of the preceding section, and under no circumstances must they be admitted to the mails.

PRECAUTIONS AGAINST INJURY TO THE MAILS.—Other articles of the fourth class which, unless properly secured, might destroy, deface, or otherwise damage the contents of the mail bag, or harm the person of any one engaged in the postal service, may be transmitted in the mails when they conform to the following conditions:

Continued on page 296.

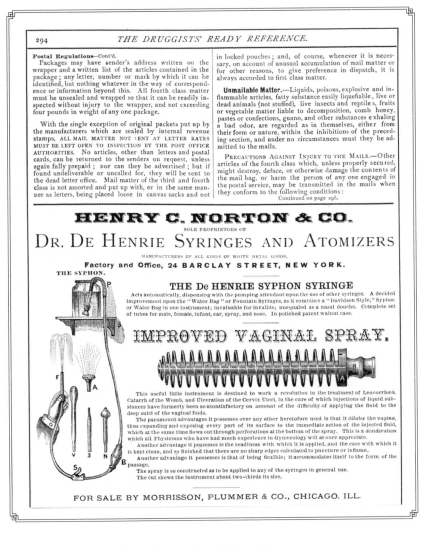
Advert for vaginal douching spray

circa 1897

A Chinaman with syphilis.

it is advised that husbands practice "continence, self-control, a willingness to deny himself . . . but a thousand voices reach us from suffering women in all parts of our land that this will not suffice; that men refuse thus to restrain themselves; that it leads to a loss of domestic happiness and to illegal amours; or that it is injurious physically and mentally—that in short, such advice is useless, because impracticable."[12] Aborting a child conceived by a man and his wife is simply not spoken of, except in hushed tones among women trading the addresses of physicians willing to perform the surgery, often ending with the death of both the mother and the fetus.

Venereal disease cures are common: advertised on public bathroom walls, matchbook covers, and by word of mouth. Syphilis causes telltale spots on the cheeks—corrosion from the inside out—but this can be easily covered up with heavily caked talc powder. Drinking mercury is thought to cure the disease, but it can make your teeth fall out. Or worse. Gentlemen who engage in this habit cover their mouth when they laugh due to embarrassment.

In Chinatown and along the Alameda Street crib line, whores go unchecked and disease is rampant. Customers are recommended to enter at their own risk.

---

12. Napheys, *The Physical Life of Woman.*

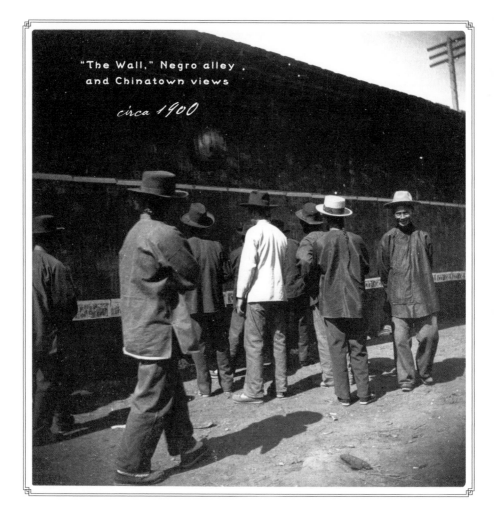

"The Wall," Negro alley
and Chinatown views

circa 1900

CHAPTER TWELVE

BALLERINO

The census lists my home country as Chile, and the papers say I am Portuguese, but I come from Milano by way of New Jersey. And I've done real nice for myself here. People think because I'm an immigrant it means I don't have the smarts, but they think wrong. It is me who controls this city. If you're looking for vice in Los Angeles, I'm the king.

I own the titles to most of the property in "Hell's Acre"—the official red-light district. Alameda Street is mine, from Marchessault to Aliso, west to Los Angeles Street. Nigger Alley crosses through my land too. And those are just my publicly listed holdings. A man likes to keep some business to himself.

It's no coincidence that when prostitution was legalized in '86 it fell within a zone of toleration on my land, exactly the site of the Alameda Street cribs. I got lots of friends in the city government

"The Wall," Negro alley
and Chinatown views

circa 1900

who owe me favors. I do trade with most of them too. Mayor "Pinky" Snyder is my silent partner in the Alameda cribs, but he don't do much except collect his take. He just sits there getting fat off my hard work, drinking his imported whiskey, and throwing his coin at high-priced cunny.

It takes brains to be an entrepreneur. I learned to do arithmetic in my head back when I was running numbers in Jersey. The first cribs I built were low-cost wood-frame row houses, with separate entrances onto the street—each single room taken by a whore charging a dollar a john. Originally I had forty crib joints, side by side. I doubled my tenancy when the Southern Pacific Railroad laid its tracks fronting Alameda in '75. Trade exploded down the block as the track workers' demand for cheap pussy mounted. Girls were pouring in from all over to fill my cribs, and plenty of the young ones born in the city too, once they started bleeding. The railroad workers would leave their lanterns in front of the cribs while they were inside with the girls—that's how it came to be known as the red-light district, anyway.

As of the end of last year, I have more than three hundred girls available to the swarms of eager customers looking for the right price—Mexican, Chinese, poor whites, and Negros who are unwelcome at the finer brothels in town. Even "respectable" men looking to save coin come to the cribs. I welcome everyone's money.

Most of my working girls are white, but you can buy Chinese, Negro, and Japanese too. We get the China girls from their homeland for the Chinamen rail workers. As for whites we have French, German, Italian, and Irish girls. People like to stick to their own kind.

Gentlemen who ain't used to fucking on this side of town complain of a lack of niceties, but I don't see no point in it. They want clean sheets and girls, they can go elsewhere. In the cribs what you see is what you get. No-frill cunny at a fair price.

Here, things are simple—a red light hangs above a large plate glass window at the front of each crib. The girls lean out of them, advertising. When they are occupied, a single sheet can be drawn closed for privacy. There's a lot of competition for the front rooms, which I let to seasoned veterans of the block. The back rooms are windowless. The rooms themselves are hardly larger than the windows fronting them with carpetless floors and bare walls. The only furniture are those of necessity: a washstand and a bed. All the extra dressing just cuts into profits.

You won't find the kind of sumptuous quarters they have in the finer palaces on New High Street or Marchessault. But I say screwing is screwing—on a gold-plated canopy or on a dirty mattress. It keeps my overhead low.

I don't have the headaches of running a house like those

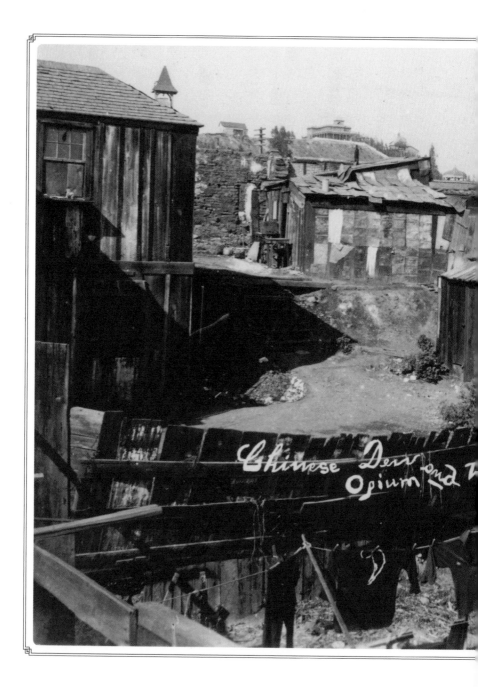

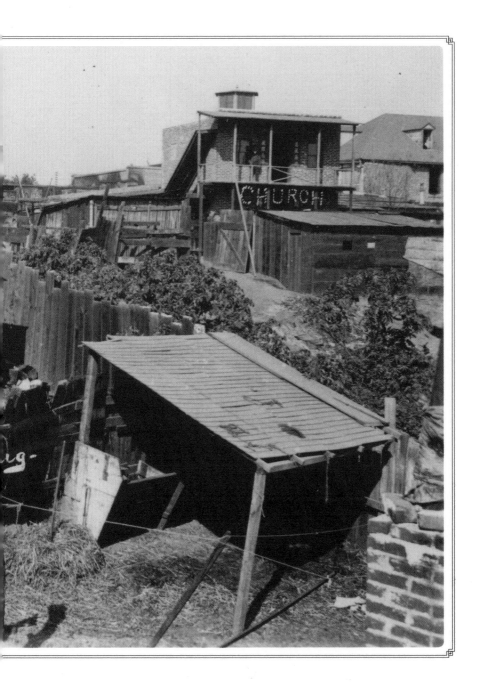

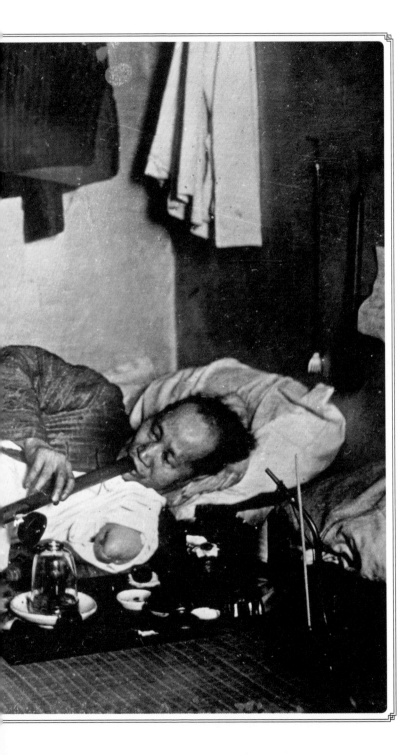

madams. I just sit back and collect daily rent of $1.50 to $2.00 from each crib girl, payable every morning, no excuses.

I added second stories onto most of my cribs and divided them up into separate rooms to capitalize on business. By packing more girls into smaller spaces, I am landlord to twenty-one inmates of the Belmont and forty-two inmates of the Arlington—and that's just two of my cribs. Not to mention the fees I charge for leasing to the Chinese and the dives on Nigger Alley.

People speculate, estimating my worth at two hundred thousand, but I'm a millionaire several times over already. And, what's better, there's no one who could even come close enough to take it from me. I keep my profits quiet. Even my wife, Maria, don't know my earnings. She's a good woman, Maria, simple. No need to worry her head with complicated multiplications.

My bosses back East thought they were taking me down a few notches, sending me to Los Angeles in '73. Thought I needed to learn more respect for the order of command. They imagined nothing out here, no prospects for a man to make good coin, that I'd be properly humbled, come back licking their boots like a good lieutenant ought to. But this town suits me good. It's been better to me than Jersey ever was, and the weather reminds me of my *amata Italia*. I have Southern California locked up in terms of trade. Boys back East keep saying they're going to visit, but Los Angeles ain't a glamorous city like Chicago and Boston—the stage stars they chase just pass through here. They're not so interested in the details of my businesses as long as their money flows. I send two hundred fifty dollars a week back to Jersey, but I'm making at least ten times that.

On top of my take from the cribs, I cash in as a saloon owner, buying liquor at wholesale cost from my own saloons. With my partner, Christopher Buckley, I co-own the Basket Saloon— it's the most popular meeting place for macs and railroad workers. In turn I supply the cribs with whiskey to sell to customers at a profit of twenty-five cents a glass. We offer a free lunch to the marks who think a lunch comes free.

The Chinese railroad workers settled on my land after they finished laying steel track, making a proper Chinatown on the bounds of my property. Now I'm landlord to their gambling parlors and opium dens too.

I make more in a night than that bitch Pearl Morton boasts she does in a fortnight. She's always talking loud, saying she got one of the largest accounts at the bank. She think she has our banker, the Fat Man, in her pocket, but he says I'm his most important client, even gave me a solid gold pen in appreciation of my business. I drop the day's take myself every evening. Don't trust no one else with my bankroll.

My hack keeps a sack of bricks in front of my carriage should I need to keep my lieutenants in line—that's how we did it in

Jersey. And to remind the girls who is boss, I keep a wooden paddle with my initials:

Bartolo Ballerino.

But out here ain't like Jersey, and I don't get to use force as often as I like. Everyone pays me proper respect except the newspapermen and the damn reformers—they're always trying to close down the crib district and save the white women from a life of vice. Reverend Sidney Kendall from Long Beach is the worst of the lot, leading the charge with his partner, Reverend Wiley Phillips. Seems like every day I'm catching it from the pulpits. They even talk of dragging me into court on some trumped-up charges of white slavery—they say they have reformed crib girls as witnesses—but I don't handle that business myself, I leave it to the French traders. Funny the reverends don't mind much about the China girls. . . . Like I said, people are only interested in their kind.

Those reverends focus their bile on me instead of the madams of the finer houses, saying the entrance to my cribs is public and the girls are outside on the streets. Those uppity madams like that dried-up quim-licker Pearl Morton think they're some kind

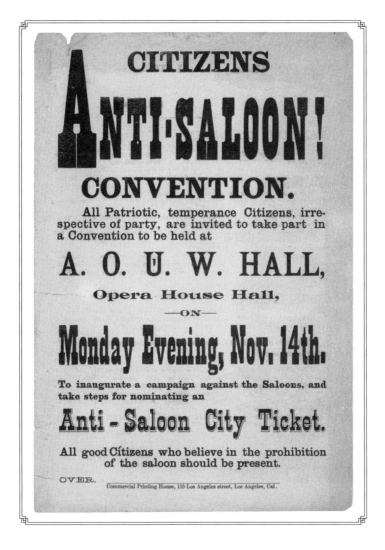

of reformers themselves, offering whores a better life just 'cause they serving supper on silver plates. I'm just providing a home for lost women too—and at such a reasonable price you'd think they'd leave me well alone.

Plaza Church, *circa 1886*

Altar boys of Plaza Church
with Rector Padre Ribena
1900

SCENES OF THE CRIB INVASION—ATTACK ON THE BASTILE.

A political cartoon from *Los Angeles Daily Times* depicting moral crusader Reverend Wiley Phillips's campaign against Ballerino's crib district. Visible in the right corner is the notorious Basket Saloon,

1903

It ain't like alternative housing in Los Angeles for wayward souls is any better. Josephine Holmes runs a boardinghouse, Belmont Hall, for sixty-odd inmates at the corner of First Street and Belmont Avenue. Just the other day I read in the Herald that she keeps her charges on a vegetarian diet, tempting them with the promise of raw meat to abate the wrath of the Devil living inside each of their souls. This lady calls herself the greatest medium of all time and gives public lectures twice weekly where she exhibits her own paintings, claiming they are executed by her paintbrush, channeled by her deceased sister's hand. I tell you, Los Angeles is full of these "mystics" and religious devotees. Bet you they turn out to be far more dangerous than us vice peddlers ever could be.

Lately it's getting so a man can't even cross the street without running into a member of the Society for the Suppression of Vice. They're zealous to shut me down but turn a blind eye to the "daytime houses," like the Manhattan, where married women meet for paid and unpaid assignations during their husbands' business hours. Even couples rent private rooms in these houses for affairs. All those upstanding men who denounce prostitution on behalf of their daughters, wives, and sisters have no trouble partaking of others' wives, daughters, and sisters in these houses.

I get reports on everything that goes on, what everyone's taste is. I'm always five steps ahead. You have to be in my trade. When I receive word the reformers are coming to visit, I get ready, hiring sign painters to construct "storefront" awnings advertising

Pete "Nigger" Johnson,
Chinatown. Preacher,
politician, & pork raiser

circa 1890

my cribs as "Corset Work," "Feathers Curled," "Fancy Work," and "Linen and Silk Handkerchiefs for Sale."

The crusaders' attacks just got us in the trade more organized. Most of the macs and pimps are now as invested in politics as I am. The French macs Pierre Lamberse, Eugene Raviere, and Maurice Alias are the most active, even got themselves matching navy blue suits to look respectable. My fellow saloon owners Felix Clevier, the Manning brothers, the Gallagher boys, and Tom Savage run a weekly meeting to keep ahead of the temperance movement. All of us profit from booze and prostitution. Better to be united in our defense against attempts to close down the district.

Those Los Angeles society women are the most vehement crusaders. They drag their skirts in the mud when crossing the street for fear of lifting their outer skirts up over their crinolines to reveal an ankle. Crib women can't afford to dirty their dresses and don't mind the advert.

In the cribs, stockings are a rarity and vanities few. Still, we got nothing on the low dives of the Tenderloin in San Francisco or the Bowery in New York. Pinky Snyder has been in the papers all month saying that Los Angeles does the best job at regulating our vice.

These purity reformers shout hail and brimstone against sin and depravity in the cribs, but I know what darkness exists in their

The Song of the Tramp

Loafing is my occupation;
The thought of toil gives me a cramp;
Work is my abomination;
I'm a regulation tramp.

I'll not work when I can get
A free-flop and a bite to eat
At some Mission, for I'm better
Satisfied my way to beat.

And such Missions, as should be known,
Work a scheme which their hall fills,
So that many tramps can be shown
To the guys that pay the bills.

Of the things which most I hate,
Saws and axes take the cake;
A Wood-yard I abominate,
Just to see one makes me ache.

The only fear my future faces
Is, that some day in this land,
There will be a lot of places
Like "Mc.Kenzie's Helping Hand."

Kindling Wood

Five Sacks for $1.00 our Specialty

360 6TH. STREET

own souls. And they're foolish to focus on moral rather than political reform—calling me names when if they knew what part their civic leaders play, their little heads would spin round.

Los Angeles's own police force is more corrupt than any of us so-called leaders of vice. Hell, I remember ten different chiefs of police between '85 and '89 alone. I give the captain and the chief of police one hundred and fifty dollars a month each to leave me be. We call the coppers "blind pigs."

From time to time the police department makes a public show of appeasing local reformers who want to barricade the red-light district and clean up the cribs. They organize monthly raids to appease the Reverend Kendall and his temperance groups, and I pay the fines myself.

Every other year some principled new recruit who doesn't know who's fronting his salary decides he's going to lead a charge against corruption and gets the newspapermen involved in his campaign. In '85, the papers were full of stories about the "Alameda Street fence question," naming Christopher Buckley and myself as the "crib kings" of Los Angeles. Buckley works for me, so I'd just like to see him try to be the king of the cribs—he'd last an hour before my boys would break that baby face. The papers accused me of refusing to donate the ground for a rear entrance alleyway behind the cribs to make our vice less visible to polite society. Some kind of tomfoolery if you ask me—I ain't donating land to no one. They can pay me with reduced interest if they want to make an offer. I can be fair. Anyway, we took care of that young man who was making all the noise.

In February this year, the chief of police made a display of arresting crib-joint girls nightly, taking them to jail, where they deposited twenty-five dollars apiece, after which they could go straight back to work. We had a little problem with one of the sergeants in the main police building on First Street between Hill and Broadway. He beat up my girls when he booked them. I had to have the chief straighten him out—I'll be the only one with the privilege of teaching my girls a lesson with the back of my paddle.

The police department was hoping the newspapers would report on the raids, placating the moral crusaders and taking the heat off city officials. The newspapers should be asking why the clients weren't arrested if you ask me. Meanwhile, six hundred dollars is sitting in the police department's bank, collecting interest.

Like the coin sitting in my vault, city funds are growing from vice too. Why, just today I was down at the Basket Saloon meeting with Pinky Snyder and the Fat Man about extending my property lines and our partnership. Pinky's going to invest city money to purchase a lot of land that just came up for sale on the east side of the tracks along Alameda. Pearl Morton was at our meet—she's always trying to horn in on our business, imagining she's got a stake in city politics, but she serves her purpose. Need

Los Angeles Chinese
Mission School faculty
1900

4762

someone's name on the land title to keep mine out of the papers. All she wants in exchange is some fresh blood for her virgin auctions. She don't think big like I do, only worries about her stupid rivalry with that Englishwoman Cora Phillips. Pearl's a silly cunt, but she knows how to make herself a nuisance. I could ruin her if I cared enough to. I collect rent from her too even if she don't know it.

The police got an effective system with the finer brothels that works good for everyone involved. Madams and girls in houses each pay monthly graft to policemen, which are kicked back to higher-ups like myself. The going rate is $14.70 to $29.70 for madams, $5.70 to $9.50 for ladies of the house. They offset the fees with the sale of beer and liquor. The police try to enforce a no-selling clause, but there's too much money to be made in booze, won't ever work to run a dry house.

My days are so full of taking care of all my holdings, I thank God for my wife, Maria. She keeps our home in order and puts a good *braciole* on the table. She give me all my little angel girls. I'm really a family man—I love my *bambinas* like nothing else. They ain't never seen the cribs and they never will. We don't live anywhere close to my businesses—I got one hundred and sixty acres of property for my homestead extending from Vermont on the west to Hoover on the east, all the way from Ninth Street to Pico. And I'm real happy there. But when Maria gets to be a pain in the ass asking questions about accounts and land titles and the little ones are crying, I take my leave.

Madams of the parlor houses are always offering me credit, but I prefer to consume in my own cribs. Most of the girls call me a ladies' man 'cause I don't much like to stick to one, though there was a time I used to.

In '79, I had a lady on the side who lived at 307 Alameda, along Little Paree. The alley is still run by Deaf Blanche, a French procuress. She keeps things in line for me down there, one of the few women I trust to handle business for me.

Ah, she was a pretty one, *la mia amante*. Clever too, like me. Made her landlady of her own crib house at No. 333–341 Alameda. Had a skylight built in, and a small garden at the back of the building, bordered by a brick wall ten feet high for privacy. Used to like sitting out there together, looking at the stars, her stroking my tensions away. It was the only time I remember feeling at peace. With her. Out there under the sky.

To keep an eye on her when I couldn't, I contracted a Frenchman, Thiebaud Bauer, to build a restaurant on the ground floor of the crib house. He cooked meals for the girls and their johns, bringing in an additional $3.50 per day in meals per person. My mind never stops thinking of ways to make coin.

Thiebaud was real useful when my wife started wondering why

I was spending so much time with the landlady. We told Maria he was my old lady's boyfriend, that shut her up good.

I really loved that lady of mine. Trusted her like I ain't never had no one. Even used to let her bring the day's profits over to my office on Second and Main Streets to deposit in my vault. Changed the combination to the letters of her name. Can't even say it no more, it hurts me so.

But June of '79, the trouble started. My lady's belly grew with child. Maria got wise after she saw Thiebaud with another woman one too many times. She threatened divorce. When a man's bank account is vulnerable, he has only one choice. I made Thiebaud swear to Maria that the kid was his and told her I'd never visit Little Paree again.

Broke my heart, it did, losing her. But it would have been broken even more if Maria had pocketed half my takings.

She delivered our son in January '80 in her rooms, with the help of Deaf Blanche, who had a newborn of her own. Heard she passed from syphilis shortly after, leaving behind our bastard child. A son. She named him Jack.

Was the hardest thing I ever had to do, to keep my distance from my own son. I used to keep an eye on Jack from afar, but I lost track of him lately, I've been so busy expanding my businesses. Was easier when he was younger—for a while there he was working as a messenger boy for Nicolas Oswald over at the

Belmont crib. He would deliver Oswald's take to Jimmy in my office, and some nights we'd pass in the hallway as I was leaving. Took everything in me not to show him favor, turn my cheek when he smiled.

Haven't laid my own eyes on him in close to a year now; he must be about seventeen, too old to do messenger boys' work—that's for street urchins from the orphan asylum on Alameda. They're useful in my trade—discreet and quick on their feet, keen to earn change for a hot meal.

You spot them fresh out of the orphanage gates, lining up to collect hot-off-the-press papers from the number of publications competing for readership—*The Los Angeles Record, The Los Angeles Evening Express, Los Angeles Herald, Los Angeles Times*, not to mention the underground and foreign-language papers. But selling papers don't pad their pockets like the extra tips we give them for delivering messages and bribes.

The same newspapers the boys dole out report on establishing a newsboys' home to keep the kids' hands clean with a roof over their heads and food on their plates. But talk is cheap. Better for a man to earn his own living is what I say. Ain't nobody held my hand when I was their age.

When he was a boy, Jack made the most tips of any of them. He was a real asset to our economy, made me proud even if he never knew. Kid grew up in the cribs. He's a native of these streets, not an immigrant like his father. And he looks just like his mother, a real beautiful boy. I could swear he has his mother's eyes and my mind for trade.

Sometimes I wonder if he's taken after me. I hear he's running trade over at Central Park for them fairy boys. But I'm sure he's like his old man with a taste for pussy. Probably knows how much money there is to be made in selling mashers—ain't much room for them down at the cribs. Like I said, real smart boy. Lately I been thinking I should look him up, see if he wants a job managing the cribs for me, help expand my interests. Be good to teach him what I learned.

Maria still ain't given me a son. Going on ten girls now—she pops out one after the other like some kind of curse. She tells me I should train our eldest, Maria Jr., in the family business, give me someone to leave my heritage to. But what use is a girl? Their place is in the home and between the sheets, and that's all there is to it.

Bartolo Ballerino,
former "king" of the red-light district, who died yesterday at a good old age.

CHAPTER THIRTEEN

ARREST RECORDS

Los Angeles Police Department Chiefs

1888 Thomas J. Cuddy
1888 L. G. Loomis
1888-1889 Hubert H. Benedict
1889 Terence Cooney
1889 James E. Burns
1889-1900 John M. Glass
1900-1904 Charles Elton

Statistics

1890 Population: 101,454
95,033 Caucasian
4,424 Chinese
1,817 Black
144 Indian
36   Japanese

1900 population: 170,298
163,975 Caucasian
6,323 Black
No records available for Chinese, Indian, or Japanese inhabitants

---

LAPD Official Report for Fiscal Year Ending April 30, 1897

Offense:

Abortion: 2 arrests, 1 conviction

Adultery: 0 arrests

Arson: 5 arrests, 5 convictions

Assault: 9 arrests, 7 convictions

Assault, Deadly Weapon: 18 arrests, 1 conviction

Begging: 57 arrests, 54 convictions

Battery: 369 arrests, 307 convictions

Burglary: 72 arrests, 34 convictions

Crime Against Nature: 2 arrests, 0 convictions

Carrying Concealed Weapons: 147 arrests, 137 convictions

Cruelty to Animals: 100 arrests, 89 convictions

Drunk: 7,758 arrests, 7,696 convictions

Los Angeles Police Department, 1895

Disturbing the Peace: 712 arrests, 615 convictions

Fire Arms, Discharging: 10 arrests, 9 convictions

Forgery: 30 arrests, 13 convictions

Gambling House, Visitors: 0 arrests

Gambling House: 215 arrests, 195 convictions

Incest: 0 arrests

Indecent Exposure: 32 arrests, 31 convictions

Ill Fame, Soliciting: 12 arrests, 12 convictions

Ill Fame, Keeping House: 22 arrests, 12 convictions

Mayhem: 2 arrests, 2 convictions

Murder: 12 arrests, 5 convictions

Opium Joint, Keeping: 2 arrests, 2 convictions

Opium Smoking: 4 arrests, 4 convictions

Rape: 26 arrests, 8 convictions

Rape, Assault to Commit: 6 arrests, 3 convictions

Robbery: 14 arrests, 3 convictions

Seduction: 1 arrest, 1 conviction

Vagrancy: 422 arrests, 384 convictions

Los Angeles Times's Reports on Prostitution-Related Arrests
In California, April 1896 to March 1897:

April 24, 1896: Crime of murder; prostitute known as "English Emma" found murdered and mutilated in a hotel room.

April 26, 1896: Crime of arson; prostitute, angry at her lover, throws a lamp, burning down the entire Cripple Creek mining camp.

July 12, 1896: Crime of sex slavery; Chinese man found guilty of importing women from China as "brides" for purposes of prostitution.

December 6, 1896: Crime of disturbing the peace; 5 prostitutes arrested for an "international brawl"–Belgian girls vs. the locals.

March 17, 1897: Crime of murder, shooting, robbery, and prostitution; Chinatown brothel.

Selected Newspaper Reports on Vice, 1902[13]

March 14: Emma Hoffman, 50, attempted suicide in one of the brothels on New High St. with a dose of morphine. Her recovery is doubtful.

June 7: It is reported that Japanese prostitutes from the Iwilei Stockdale in Hawaii are being imported to Los Angeles for local cribs.

June 11: The Vienna Buffet is under municipal fire for permitting their chorus girls to fraternize with the big spenders in their dressing rooms.

August 13: John Karnell, a "mac" or pimp, was arrested for being drunk and a vagrant. He was the best-dressed vagrant in jail, however, and had enough money on his person to bail out several vagrants.

September 9: Justo Morales, a Cuban negro, was arrested for trying to sell a pair of women's shoes he had stolen. He attempted to sell them to some Alameda St. girls.

October 15: Annie Brady of 142 $\frac{1}{2}$ N. Main St. tried suicide. Deserted by her husband, she had become a prostitute. Feeling disgraced she swallowed poison, later morphine.

November 17: E. M. Campbell, a cripple, cut a sailor with a knife at the Basket Saloon on Alameda St. Campbell was the piano player at the Basket.

---

13. Excerpted from W. W. Robinson papers, "Alameda Street Notes," 1902-1904, courtesy of UCLA Special Collections.

December 2: Effie Russell of the Stella Mitchell sporting house at 540 New High St. tried suicide with carbolic acid. She had been working there for three months, and had come from Denver, where her parents still live.

December 16: E.M. Campbell, legless piano player of the Basket Saloon, was given 60 days for the assault on Jon View, the sailor, who fancied himself a joker. The affair ". . . included 'ladies' and drinks."

Selected Reports on Vice, 1903[14]

January 20: Josie Botto, 16, was taken from a bawdy house on Marchessault Street and placed with the police matrons.

January 26: Two young boys and two young girls were arrested when they tried to obtain a room at the "Euclid" on N. Main.

February 7: "Two pretty little Japanese girls," Yuwu and Hana Naritomi, have been put into the Ransome home. They were kidnapped in Japan and sold for immoral purposes. Their alleged stepfather, K. Naritomi, no longer has any control over them as they are over 16. They were rescued by the Japanese Society for Improvement of Morals and will be sent back to Japan.

February 13: Carrie Nation headed a delegation to visit the cribs on Alameda St. accompanied by the Chinatown police. A crowd of about 100 men and boys followed the party. At least 100 women were in Ballerino's Alley and some listened to her speech.

April 28: An ordinance prohibiting boys under 17 in saloons, pool halls, and houses of ill fame has been proposed.

May 15: The Door of Hope Mission for fallen women was dedicated at 119 N. Daly. The matron is to be Mrs. Phillebar.

---

14. Excerpted from W. W. Robinson papers, "Alameda Street Notes," 1902-1904, courtesy of UCLA Special Collections.

May 19: The ordinance prohibiting boys under 17 from entering houses of ill repute was passed.

June 12: Lodging houses and houses of ill fame which sell liquor face penalties unless they pay city license fees. Liquor in these places has been sold in increasing amounts.

July 6: A Mexican named Montijo died of strychnine poisoning by eating candy treated with strychnine on Alameda Street.

July 7: Montijo died of drink, not strychnine poisoning, say the examining doctors.

September 12: Lou Fletcher, inmate of a brothel at 327 Aliso St., took an antiseptic as poison. She was taken to the hospital and returned when she was considered out of danger. She said she took the poison to "see how it tasted."

October 2: Madge Moore, one of the red-light girls, took some laudanum in her beer at the Center Saloon, 106 W. Court St. Though she became very sick she was out of danger later on.

October 2: A man named Bert Henry, about 35, was arrested in the Plaza. He was well dressed and had a dope kit on him. Although he claimed to have been using the stuff for 15 years, he didn't look dope-ravaged as one might expect.

December 9: Ella Powers was shot and wounded by Michael Walsh because she wanted to quit prostituting herself and become respectable. Walsh was living off her earnings and evidently saw his livelihood threatened. Earlier, on Nov. 24, he had cut her with a knife. Ella lives in the St. Lawrence Lodging House at $656\frac{1}{2}$ S. Main.

December 10: Myrtle Richards, a schoolgirl, has run away from home. Though she is only 13, she has a man friend who is 21, and it is feared he has lured her away to live a life of shame. Earlier she had shown some gold coins to some friends and said that they were given to her by a "friend." Her father is a carpenter who lives on Carondelet between 7th and 8th Sts.

CHAPTER FOURTEEN

X

Try as I might, I cannot shake the insomnia that has plagued me for some forty-odd years. I have come to embrace its endless hours, awake, my brain buzzing. When I finally do close my dry, twitching eyes for a few precious hours of slumber, they are restless, filled with dreams that remind me of people and places I've long discarded. I wake every morning feeling as though something has been taken from me. It is difficult to pinpoint exactly what.

Most nights my dreams are the same.

I am a young boy, wandering in dense woods, led by a peculiar humming, a distorted buzzing sound in my ears. It is louder now and I can almost make out a woman's voice whispering in the drone, though her words are impossible to decipher. Without noticing my path, I find myself in a clearing, surrounded by an herb garden I had once stumbled upon on an outing with my mother.

A young woman is bent over the rows, picking leaves of plants I can't recognize from my botany books. From the edge of the clearing I watch her, the nape of her neck exposed, tendrils of hair loose from her bonnet. A cream blouse slips off her milky shoulders, no sign of a corset. Slowly, she turns toward me as though she was aware of my presence but allowed my stare. She smiles, her eyes black and glittering. We do not speak aloud, but I feel as if my thoughts are being invaded.

Purring an impenetrable tune, she beckons to me. I follow her down a winding path to a large oak tree, its trunk revealing a small hut, constructed out of leaves camouflaging its exterior. Together, we enter. Inside is a small room, furnished with a single mat on the floor made from grasses and straw.

The woman turns away from me again, leisurely untying her bonnet, shaking loose a tumble of shiny long black hair. Her hands go next to her waist, unfastening the buttons on her dress. She lets it fall to the floor. I am rooted to my spot, utterly transfixed—unable to move my limbs to touch her or to open my mouth to speak. She wears a loose white gown underneath, and I can see the outline of her buttocks through the thin gauze. I notice her bare feet are absent of dirt from the garden. As my mind starts to wander, she bends forward, gathering up her dress with both hands, lifting it up over her head. She stands still, her back to me, as I admire her nakedness. Like a swan gliding through a pond, she crosses the room and reclines on the mat in one fluid movement. Her gleaming black eyes, devoid of expression, call forth. With a long finger, she summons me to her. All rational thought disappears.

I am standing atop a mountain overlooking the sea. Just beyond is a land I have never seen. There is a deafening thunder, but the skies are cloudless blue. The noise intensifies. I turn around and see a low mist inching toward me, it envelops me completely.

And then I am awake and she is gone. My trousers are wet and my skin burns. And all day long I cannot forget her.

I've had the nightmares since childhood, regularly awakened by my own screams in the middle of the night, to find myself alone, in my cold room in the English countryside, my governess running in with a glass of water, giving a perfunctory "There, there," and leaving as quickly as she had arrived. Mother never appeared to comfort me, believing, like most of our class, that children should be seen and not heard.

I was left to soothe myself, guiding my hands underneath my nightshirt, stroking softly between my thighs. My pubescent member rose like a horn while I whispered "There, there" to myself over and over. Only after I'd excreted my spunk was I able to fall back asleep.

As the years have given way, sleep has become almost unbearable, my dreams vivid and bottomless. Each morning I awake in a cold sweat. It has only gotten worse since I've come to this city. Los Angeles. The desert chill leaves my bones aching for more warmth than the hearth provides, and I find the dry heat of the days makes my disquiet even more pronounced.

My dreams have traveled with me, across an ocean and a new continent, accompanying me here, where I am as far away as I can be from almost everyone who remembers me. Not that many care to. The ones I have left behind wish only to forget. I welcome my nightmares, like I do my insomnia, as my oldest friends.

Some visit mediums, palmists, healers, to interpret their dreams. Especially so here in this city—the recent census lists six of them on Spring Street between First and Temple alone:

———————————————————

Margaret Mayhaim, "Magnetic Healer"
Boarder, 46 years old
1 child

Emily White, "Card Reader"
Head of home, emigrated England 1884, widowed
Bore 7 children, 4 still living

Marguerite Smith, "Actress"
22 years old, emigrated France via Georgia

Mimette Smith, "Actress"
19 years old, emigrated France via Georgia

Lulu Walker, "Palmist"
33 years old, married 15 years

Annabel Hudson, "Beauty Doctor"
45 years old, emigrated England 1875
1 child

Flora Howard, "Author"
Boarder, 48 years old, widowed

Mary E. W. Wright, "Medium"
Lodger, 71 years old, married
Bore 6 children, 3 still living

Antoinette Bowen, "Masseuse"
Lodger, 34 years old, emigrated Germany
Married 18 years

Emma Richards, "Dressmaker"
33 years old, widowed
Bore 2 children, both deceased
7 mos. unemployed

Gussie Swedenborg, "Clairvoyant"
33 years old, emigrated Sweden, widowed
1 child, deceased

Ella M. Thornton, "Embalmer"
Single woman, 31 years old

Mrs. Emma F. Danello, "Literary Writer"
Boarder, 38 years old, widowed

Miss Marta Abadi Lodge, "Income from Parents"
25 years old

Viola Packard, "Palmist"***
Divorced, 34 years old
2 children, deceased
201 N. Spring Street
***Spiritual Readings
10 AM to 4 PM daily

They ply their trade on countless fools who think they can control their fate. But it is impossible to escape one's own destiny. I suppose that is the American way, though. Rising from circumstances, pulling oneself up with one's bootstraps, and all the self-fulfilling prophecies they speak of here. Back in England a man knows his place and stays there.

My family seat, a stone estate in the county of Wiltshire, England, has been ours for centuries. At my birth, it belonged to my maternal grandfather. My grandmother had been a lady-in-waiting to Queen Victoria in her youth. She died long before I was born. My mother was a bored lady of the house. My father left for the Crimean War when I was only an infant. He never returned. And my grandfather, the patriarch of our great house, was mostly away in London, spending our fortune on women, spirits, and his treasured books.

19th-century "spirit" photograph.
Mediums and spirit photographers
superimposed "ghostly" images atop their
clients' portraits to provide proof of their
supernatural abilities.

Although my ancestors' portraits lined the long hallways of our home and should have reminded me of my proud lineage, I felt nothing but their cold dead stares. I often stopped in front of my father's portrait, looking for a resemblance, but I could never find one. My days were otherwise spent alone in darkened nursery rooms while Mother entertained in her quarters. She had no inclination to entertain me.

Mother. She is always with me: a ghostly vision in the backdrop of my memories.

She had little time for me, but I adored her—every last detail of her face, her hands, her smell. I still keep a small, worn photograph of her in my breast pocket, stolen from a picture frame in the study back in Wiltshire long ago. It is all I have left to connect me to a woman I barely knew. The last time I saw her I was twelve.

Even then it was uncommon to come across her in our enormous, lonely house. She was always occupied in her drawing room with her gentlemen callers, the door locked from the inside. I used to hear the staff whispering about Mother's guests, though they fell silent when they sensed my presence. I don't think I even saw the inside of her rooms until I was seven.

It was late January, around my birthday, which I'd celebrated with the cook, Mrs. Baxter, and a large buttercream cake, in the kitchen. Mother was out riding. I stole into her rooms, prying open the door with a hairpin she'd once dropped on the nursery floor. Her receiving room looked like any other in the house: a sitting room with a fireplace, a chaise longue, and small table in the center. Her bedroom connected via a small door and was furnished with a blue-canopied bed in the center. A folding Japanese dressing screen was open against one wall, next to a pale pink Louis XIV armoire and dresser set edged in gilt with a golden mirror above.

I went first to the armoire, struck by her scent, still lingering among the silk gowns and velvet robes, as I opened its heavy doors. I spent several minutes with my head buried inside, inhaling deeply with my eyes shut, as though to invoke her presence.

Next, I went to the dresser, with a silver hairbrush and a set of crystal bottle atomizers laid on top. I ran my fingers over the bristles of her brush, pausing to extract a few strands of her long brown hair and carefully wrapped them inside my handkerchief.

I opened the top drawer of the dresser first: piles of lace bloomers, neatly folded in rows. The second drawer held pink and cream corsets, lying lengthwise across. The bottom drawer was locked. I jimmied the keyhole with her hairpin until I heard a click.

I pulled aside a piece a cloth that covered the contents of the drawer to reveal a set of books. The top one was leather-bound and stamped in gilt: *Fairie Tales*. I opened up the cover, reading the inscription to my mother in my grandfather's scrawl: "*To my darling daughter on her 7th birthday,*" I turned the brittle pages of text, written in Old English, which I couldn't read, to several color plates of illustrations. They weren't like the ones in the fairy tales my governess read to me. These had beast-men with horned heads ravaging maidens while shriveled old witches looked on.

I put the book aside. Below were three wooden boxes tied together with rope with an envelope resting on top. I untied the knot and carefully unfolded the letter inside: *To my daughter upon the occasion of her 15th birthday.* Each box featured sliding panels, carved on the top with a scene of a Japanese woman—cooking, cleaning, and arranging flowers. I slid the first one open—the woman was not cooking dinner, she was on the floor with a man inside her, his body wedged between her thighs, her legs akimbo on either side of her and hair undone. I wasn't sure I wanted to open the next. Even now, I remember my stomach feeling queasy.

And then the sound of muffled voices coming from the other room. I quickly put the boxes back, knowing my bottom would be sore from the spanking I'd receive if caught. In the mirror above the dresser, I could see that the door to the sitting room was being opened—Mother was back early from her ride.

There wasn't time enough to sneak away—I hid behind the dressing screen. Then Mother's footsteps came into the bedroom, followed by another set. She was not alone. I peeked through the slit in the screen. A man, Mr. ——. I'd seen him before, as he often visited the house.

"Do you need to check on the boy?"

"He's fine. The governess has him well handled."

"Mmmmm, a boy needs his mother . . ."

Then they didn't speak anymore. The next sounds that came were moans. I shut my eyes and covered my ears.

I must have spent hours crouched behind the screen, trying to block out Mother's screams. To pacify myself, I silently hummed a lullaby Mother sang to herself when she thought no one was near:

Beneath the weeping willows
Where sorrow seldom grows
A lady of the forest
As pure as driven snow

I repeated the refrain until the words disappeared and a steady hum drowned out all other thoughts. Finally, there was no noise at all. Mother and Mr. —— were quiet. A pale moon shone brightly through the open window. Mr. —— snored.

I crept from my hiding place and tiptoed through the bedroom with painstaking footsteps so as not to disturb their slumber, averting my eyes as I passed the bed. Halfway to the door I stopped, unable to resist looking back at Mother's naked body splayed across the sheets, Mr. ——'s head resting on her thighs. She opened her eyes and looked directly at me. She didn't say anything; she just smiled.

The incident was never discussed.

After that my self-abuse became all-consuming. Morning, afternoon, and in the schoolroom during lessons, I'd rub my Man Thomas until I came, so much so that my skin was red and irritated at bathtime. My nursemaids pretended not to notice; they preferred not to discuss my troubling behavior out loud. They told each other in whispers that it wasn't their place to teach me about such things.

My emissions were the only moments of peace I had in that old house, a consoling release in place of familial embraces. Endless tutors left as quickly as they arrived, saying something was wrong with me, that the house felt odd, with its strange corridors opening into rooms that weren't meant to exist. Grandfather was an amateur draftsman and drew the unusual additions to the house himself. Bedrooms had windows that peered onto others, like convex mirrors. Hidden panels behind walls hung with tapestries revealed secret architecture, doors connecting parts of the house to others. One felt unseen eyes monitoring their movements.

When Grandfather was in residence, he was sequestered in his library. Like Mother's rooms, his doors remained locked. I had broken in once, just once, when Grandfather was away in London to look at a book collection. It was the most beautiful room I had ever seen. The walls were painted a deep rich red. Cases of bookshelves, floor to ceiling. A set of iron shackles hung casually against the wall in the corner. I felt safe there.

Grandfather died from inflammation of the bowels when I was

fifteen, likely brought on by years of debauchery and drunkenness. When his will was read, I learned that he had left me the country seat and his library's contents, along with a healthy yearly sum. Mother disappeared shortly thereafter. Freed from my governess's watch, I spent my hours devouring Grandfather's collection.

It was an odd assortment of books, cataloged by subject matter: alchemy, astronomy, bestiality, botany, egyptology . . . witch-craft. The eroticus section was the most complete. Several volumes were more than four hundred years old, from as far away as Japan, India, and France. In the center bookcase of the library, taking up eight entire shelves, were a cache of "sporting guides": private guidebooks to Europe's finest houses of pros-titution. *Pretty Women of Paris; London's Haymarket Whores; Venetian Courtesans; Guidebook to Geisha; Delicacies of the Sultan's Harem; Slave Girls of Ancient Greece; Directory to the Seraglios in New York, Philadelphia, Boston, and All the Princi-pal Cities in the Union.*

Some of these were kept in their own glass cases, too old and fragile to be touched without gloves. The European ones dated back to 1649, separate slim books for each year and country. They were all privately printed and simply bound with the edi-tion and distribution of copies stamped on their inside cover.

Inside the pages were records of for-profit sexual services. Madams were cataloged by address, and the ladies of their houses were listed by name below. A brief description followed: hours open, prices charged, drinks served, and specialties of the house defined. There were separate entries for women who operated independently. These were sometimes as vague as "Lizzie, a bargain for a sixpence: 7–4 AM; south side of Thames, off Tooley Street, under the 2nd gaslight." Others were written in such complimentary prose that it appeared as though it were a paid advertisement. The American ones took the most liberty with this style:

MRS. JENNY CASWELL

This is one of the most fashionable retreats in the city. The lady hostess accommodates some ten beautiful, charming lady boarders who will vie with any we have ever seen. Miss Anna Lawrence is the belle of this mansion. Mrs. Caswell keeps the very best wines the markets afford, and gents from the West will find here a home to realize their dreams of matrimony in comfort, splendor, and luxury. Mrs. C is courteous, agreeable, polite, and entertaining, and well knows how to accommodate visitors.

Some brothels and girls were listed year after year, address changes noted, and services added. Others made only the briefest of appearances before disappearing into obscurity, dying from disease or murder, their bodies most likely dumped into shallow water.

Grandfather's notations marked the pages. Places he had been to personally had roman numerals indicating the number of visits—an asterisk next to a name indicated a favored girl.

Illustration from Harris' List, or Cupid's London directory, an 18th-century sporting guide published annually from 1757 to 1795.

I spent months on end locked in the library as Grandfather had, reading his guides over and over, deciphering his pencil marks in the margins, cross-referencing illustrations so that I could better picture the sorts of women who had surrendered to Grandfather's prowess. I barely ate or slept, so consumed was I by my books.

Every few weeks I sent away to my grandfather's favorite book-seller in London, Mr. Littleton, to replenish my supply of the latest ideas set forth in science, medicine, and the erotic arts. Sometimes a new sporting guide would be included in the pack-ages. For these I paid dearly. Years passed.

By my eighteenth birthday, I'd grown tired of country life, my mind awakened by the knowledge of what lay beyond the bor-ders of my grounds. And so I ventured out of my library to the city for the first time. The stench of London, the crowds in the Haymarket, the low Cockney slang—all were an affront to my senses. But still I persisted, drawn to visit the places I'd read about in the guides myself. In the Haymarket alone there were countless offerings: Kate Hamilton's rooms for private assig-nations; dancing girls at the Portland rooms; sailors' preferred brothels on Frederick and Brunswick Streets in a dangerous area known as Tigers Bay. I tried these too.

For a time, the whores replaced my appetite for self-pleasure—my agony of bliss bringing me back each time to my childhood bedroom, Mother's voice uttering words she'd never spoken in a soft whisper: "There, there." And then just as quickly the sensation would pass and it was onto the next. A continual hunt for an elusive high.

I marked the guides with my own notations—contraceptives used, diseases common, places to avoid—filling several of my own notebooks in the first year alone. A large bribe to the madams of the finer establishments helped smooth my way to unlimited access. I considered my research to be highly disciplined and more thorough than my grandfather's, as I tested drinks, food, rooms, and maid service, recording my impressions of decor and ambience. I even conducted personal interviews with the inmates of the houses to learn their patois. There was also the business of sampling the women. I inputted each conquest in neatly ordered rows of ink, with ruler-drawn margins separating the columns. I never slept with the same woman more than three times, finding they grew too attached, and I, too bored, preferred to move on.

I wore a black cape and a hat pulled low over my face to avoid prying eyes, taking back-alley routes to circumvent gaslit streets. The better houses had separate entrances for clients wishing to preserve anonymity. I left behind only my calling card: a thick cream stock stamped with my initial.

X

I passed most of my second decade this way, haunting the city's establishments, with brief visits to Wiltshire to recover in solitude, each time more weary, my heart heavier. I began to crave something greater, someone who could save me from the monotony of my wanderings, but I could not foresee finding anyone who could equal my all-consuming desire for the next release.

Soon I tired of London and went abroad on the continent, to visit the brothels of France and Italy. Grandfather was much beloved by the whores in Paris, and I found some of their daughters still working. In Paris, I met the infamous courtesan Cora Pearl, born Emma Crouch, who was so bold as to serve herself naked on a platter to her dinner guests. Every day there was another whore to try.

More years passed.

Climaxing grew harder to achieve. The great effort it took left me feeling little sense of ease anymore. I tried herbal potions and everything that one could sample—orgies, male students paid handsomely to gratify me in the secrecy of a dark alley, masochistic madams who showed pain in place of pleasure. Nothing, no one, could satisfy my desire; more often than not I ended my trysts flaccid and alone.

Even more years went by. At thirty-nine, a two-month sojourn in Italy to visit Simonetta de la Conterno, the notorious Italian courtesan, so weakened my constitution that I contracted

a severe bout of tuberculosis. It took months to recover, lying in bed, unable to continue my research. Our family doctor suggested that I might try a drier climate to clear out my lungs; he thought I could use a long rest.

California had recently developed an international reputation as a place for recuperation. It served another purpose too. My family name was too well known in Europe, and rumors were rampant about my nocturnal wanderings. My accountants, alarmed by my reckless spending, said that if I was to continue my research, I'd have to consider alternate sources of income—I was eating into the capital of my estate.

A.C.VR

Vroman's Bookstore in Pasadena
1896

And so here I am, in Los Angeles, lying on my couch in another library, thousands of miles away from anyone I know . . . almost anyone.

Except for Cora, my perfect little prize. Besides Edwin, my valet, and my books, of course, she is my only treasure from home. I found her when she was just a little waif, sweeping floors for Mr. Littleton, my book dealer in London. For a while, it amused me to have her as my plaything, but she was brighter than any woman I had ever met, and had an appetite for books that almost matched my own. I took it upon myself to educate her—a combination of finishing-school etiquette and training in London's finest brothels. Once she was polished, she was almost ideal.

And now, in Los Angeles, she serves a purpose more valuable than ever—it is her records I go over nightly, here in my private library—strewn with the chaos of my new business. My floor is scattered with parchment papers, filled with drawings and handwritten scrolls. Piles of books are stacked precariously high and topped with piles of yellowed newspaper clippings and photographic prints. My desk is covered with official documents: land purchase records, receipts, and bank deposits stamped CLASSIFIED.

I've been industrious in my new hometown. In place of my neat little notebooks are new diaries crammed with crossed-out lines

SCIENTIFIC AMERICAN

[Entered at the Post Office of New York, N. Y. as Second Class matter.]

A WEEKLY JOURNAL OF PRACTICAL INFORMATION, ART, SCIENCE, MECHANICS, CHEMISTRY, AND MANUFACTURES.

Vol. LXXVI.—No. 16.
Established 1845.

NEW YORK, APRIL 17, 1897.

[$3.00 A YEAR.
WEEKLY.

Fig. 1.—THE DARK ROOM AND REEL FOR DEVELOPING FILMS.

Fig. 2.—THE BIOGRAPH AT WORK IN A NEW YORK THEATER.

Fig. 3.—INTERIOR OF THE "MUTOSCOPE."

Fig. 4.—THE "MUTOGRAPH" PHOTOGRAPHING THE PENNSYLVANIA LIMITED WHEN RUNNING AT THE RATE OF SIXTY MILES AN HOUR.

PHOTOGRAPHY AS AN ADJUNCT TO THEATRICAL REPRESENTATION.—[See page 248.]

Offices of Wilshire
Magazine

May, 1906

and missing pages. My guidebooks have changed since coming to America; there is more at stake now.

I have become an investor.

It was a matter of economics—prostitution is the world's oldest profession and possibly the most lucrative commercial industry. One can make a killing if one operates correctly.

And where better to do so than in Los Angeles? New York, Chicago, and Boston all have established prostitution districts. I have read and sampled these cities' guides and know their vice to be controlled by well-oiled machinery. Los Angeles is a city so far removed from the cultural centers of this country that one could be forgotten or build their own dreams. Merchants of all sorts occupy our city center, serving a fast-growing population—my findings count close to two hundred thousand new inhabitants.

The flesh trade is thriving—I have made a fortune matching my yearly income in the last two months alone. But Cora doesn't share my delight at our success. I've given her everything she could want—even the plum position as madam of our own house, the Golden Lion, but it is not enough for her. I have to wonder what the point of my life's work is if I've no one to leave it all to, no heir who cares enough to follow in my footsteps? It is these thoughts lately that gnaw at my insides, through endless days and endless nights.

I rub my tired eyes, knowing I've a full evening of work ahead. Pour myself another drink from the decanter beside my couch. Make my way across the room to my favorite seat by the window overlooking my garden. Settle in, removing a roll of papers from my inside jacket pocket, frowning as I decipher my scrawl.

It's taken me the better part of this year to compile my findings—and prepare this, my first published effort, a complete sporting guide to Los Angeles. I've started many others—in London, Rome, Paris—tossing each one away, unsatisfied. Those cities are already overrun with little black guidebooks. No, I want to be the first to charter this territory, out here in the western-most state. And now, my masterwork is almost ready—only my foreword remains to be written.

As these plates are being readied for printing, a formal introduction is in order. I shall attempt to clarify my intent with this booklet, though I am hardly sure that I will manage it so neatly as to appease. Thoughts drip from my pen—not a drizzle but a downpour, a torrential flood, the likes of which this city so rarely sees. My sentences dissipate once becoming ink on paper, washed away by my own hand. . . .

I am trapped inside a body I do not inhabit. My skin feels rubbery, numb. I see, I hear, I touch, but I do not feel. I place my digits upon a surface, but I have no reaction. I do not judge those basest of thoughts and actions; I am simply devoid of them myself.

To assume I am detached from my subjects—the women and men who populate this guide—is only partially true. I have a deeper understanding of them—their routines, pain, and loving—than perhaps they do of themselves. It is not with arrogance that I speak, I state only what I have documented through years of study.

I wander through streets, dark alleys uniform in their monotony, geography fades; each gutter smells and looks the same. In every corner of this muck and mire it is inescapable to recognize the hardness around the mouth and in the gaze of women accustomed to earning their living through the company they keep.

I present here my private directory of this city of lost angels. A highly classified and thoroughly cataloged listing of specimens: names, locations, and prices sought.

This public service is indeed necessary to any growing metropolis. If Los Angeles is to ever compete with the urban centers of the world—those being at the present time New York, Boston, Chicago, and San Francisco—it is imperative for such a guide to exist. For what is a city without its vices?

Having set forth these notes, I wonder whether I shall deliver these pages to the printer after all. Perhaps my observations should remain private, unseen by those who would not, could not, understand.

Likely I shall toss this manuscript into the fire, as I have so many others, another record destroyed. Los Angeles grows so quickly that by the time this booklet is distributed it will be rendered obsolete, the buildings I speak of demolished, all traces of a world once alive gone. To capture a single moment in time in this city seems a futile effort, for its people have no desire to remember even the recent past.

—July 1897, Los Angeles

LOS ANGELES

———————————•———————————

1781 Los Angeles is founded as *El Pueblo de Nuestra Senora la Reina de los Angeles de Porciuncula* or the Town of Our Lady of Angels of the Porciuncula River.

1804 Morphine is isolated from opium.

1848 The California Gold Rush starts after nuggets of the rich ore are found at Sutter's Mill in Coloma.

1850 Thanks to the Compromise of 1850, California enters the Union as the thirty-first state.

1850s Los Angeles earns the nickname "Los Diablos" due to the high amount of murders (forty-four murders in thirteen months with no convictions).

1854 The first schoolhouse is built by the city on the northwest corner of Spring and Second Streets.

1856 The first orphanage in Los Angeles is established by the Daughters of Charity of St. Vincent de Paul, on the corner of Alameda and Macy Streets (the current site of Union Station).

1865 John G. Downey builds a two-story brick mansion with a private ballroom at the northwest corner of Fourth and Main Streets.

1869 Two- and three-story brick buildings begin replacing adobes in downtown Los Angeles.

October 24, 1871 More than five hundred whites and Latinos raid Negro Alley and kill nineteen Chinese men and boys in the "Chinese Massacre."

1873 The Comstock Act is voted into law. Largely the work of Victorian vice hunter Anthony Comstock, the law prohibits mailing information or articles related to contraception, abortion, or erotica.

1873-1874 The first railroad tracks are installed in downtown Los Angeles, servicing Main Street to Spring Street; First Street to Fort Street (now Broadway); Fourth Street, Hill Street, Sixth Street to Pearl Street (now Figueroa).

1874 The first municipal streetcar begins service.

May 27, 1874 Prostitution is outlawed in Los Angeles's central business district.

1876 With the arrival of the Southern Pacific Railroad, Los Angeles is linked to the transcontinental rail system.

1877 Dr. Elizabeth A. Follanbee becomes the first female practitioner of medicine in Los Angeles.

1877 *Calle de los Negros* (known locally as "Nigger's Alley" or "Nigger Alley") is renamed Los Angeles Street.

1879 The Los Angeles Athletic Club is founded.

1880 Main Street north of First becomes the first stretch of roadway to be paved with cement and asphalt.

1881 The *Los Angeles Daily Times* newspaper begins publication.

February 1881 Snow falls on the streets of Los Angeles.

1882 The telephone is introduced to Los Angeles.

December 31, 1882 Electric streetlamps are introduced to Los Angeles. Gas companies started an opposition campaign claiming that electric light attracted bugs, contributed to blindness, and had a bad effect on ladies' complexions. The lamps are not operated on moonlit nights due to complaints.

1882 Chinese immigration to the United States is barred in the Chinese Exclusion Act.

1883 Fannie Bernstein becomes the first female graduate of Los Angeles High School to enter the University of California.

1883 The railroad links the Gulf of Mexico to the Pacific Ocean (New Orleans to Los Angeles).

1884 The city of Los Angeles pays fifty thousand dollars to Colonel Griffith J. Griffith for his rights to the Los Angeles River water.

1884 D. W. Child opens Child's Opera House on Main Street, south of First Street. It is the first theater of consequence downtown, with a capacity of eighteen hundred.

October 1884 *Le Progres,* Los Angeles's first French-language publication, begins circulation.

1885 Electric streetcar lines go in along Los Angeles and San Pedro Streets. They stretch down Maple Avenue to Pico Boulevard.

March 1885 Sewing is introduced to the curriculum in Los Angeles's public schools.

1885 Dorothea Lummis settles in Los Angeles, becomes president of the Los Angeles Homeopathic Medical Society, and later founds the Society for the Prevention of Cruelty to Children.

1885-1889 Ten different men serve as chief of police in four years' time.

1886 Chief of Police Edward McCarthy is removed from office for "irregularities."

1886 A segregated vice district is ordained between Third and High Streets and west of Alameda Street. Prostitution is legalized within this zone of toleration.

1886 Railroad wars entice those headed to California with cheap fares and promises of inexpensive land. At one point rates fall to one dollar for round-trip travel from Los Angeles to the Missouri River.

1886 There are one thousand and fifty telephones in use in Los Angeles.

1886 Edwin Cawston opens the United States's first ostrich farm in Arroyo Seco between Pasadena and Los Angeles to help meet the demand for feather plumes in high-fashion hats.

1887 Ranch owner and prohibitionist Harvey Wilcox founds "Hollywood."

1887 The real estate craze begins in earnest in Los Angeles.

1887 The population of Los Angeles is listed at near sixty thousand, but the telephone directory only lists eighteen thousand adults.

1887 Guests pay fifty cents (a quarter for kids) to see a massive indoor panorama of the Siege of Paris on Main Street between Third and Fourth Streets.

March 1, 1887 The Women's Home opens on Fourth Street to the benefit of women and girls out of employment.

1888 The Los Angeles Theater is built on Spring Street between Second and Third Streets.

1888 The Southern Pacific suspends service to its River Station as the magnificent palm-lined Arcade Station opens at Fourth and Alameda Streets.

November 9, 1888 The sensational and gory deaths of London prostitutes in the Whitechapel murders achieve worldwide fame as Jack the Ripper slays his final victim.

1888-1890 Heavy rains lead to catastrophic flooding.

1889 To combat the scale insect, whose effect on citrus groves is devastating, the ladybug is introduced to Los Angeles, with great success.

July 1, 1890 Elijah Bond markets the first Ouija board.

August 1891 Pearl Morton opens her brothel in a building once home to the Los Angeles Superior Court.

1892 Edward Doheny discovers oil in Los Angeles at the corner of Colton and Patton Streets.

1893 Four Los Angeles banks close due to a nationwide economic slump.

1893 The Bradbury building, built with iron materials from France and the first elevators in Los Angeles, opens at Third Street and Broadway.

July 29, 1893 The Atchison, Topeka, and Santa Fe railroad opens its Moorish-designed Le Grande Station at the corner of Santa Fe and Second Streets.

1894 The Pullman strike shuts down railroads across the country while labor riots break out in Los Angeles.

1895 The current Wilshire Boulevard is named just west of downtown.

1895 Josephine Holmes founds Belmont Hall, a boarding school for ladies. A *Los Angeles Times* article from February 17, 1895, describes it as a "queer institution," where sixty-odd "inmates" are slaves to Miss Holmes.

1895 Police constables crusade against Alameda Street cribs ("dollar-joint" prostitution).

1896 The Sherman & Clark electric railroad goes from downtown Los Angeles to Santa Monica.

1897 Cora Phillips's Golden Lion brothel opens for business on Alameda Street. Two stone lions guard the entrance.

1897 Madame Bolanger's Octoroon brothel begins operation.

1897 Belle Newell is arrested for "soliciting" and charged a ten-dollar fine.

1897 The last horse car disappears from Los Angeles as the Main Street line becomes electric.

1897 The first automobile appears in Los Angeles.

1898 Los Angeles's first Chinese-language newspaper, *Wah Mei Sun Po*, goes to print.

1898 Los Angeles forms its own symphony (the fifth in the nation).

1898 William Mulholland is named the first superintendent of the Los Angeles Department of Water and Power.

1899 The breakwaters at San Pedro Harbor is constructed to facilitate the building of a new port of Los Angeles.

1903 William Randolph Hearst establishes the *Los Angeles Examiner*.

1905 A liquor license is awarded to the Golden Gopher bar in downtown Los Angeles.

1908 The Los Angeles district attorney closes Pearl Morton's house.

1908 The grand jury investigation of Mayor Arthur Harper's connections examines his relationship with local brothels.

1908 Located just over a mile apart, Philippe's and Cole's Pacific Electric Buffet each claim to have invented the French dip sandwich to rave customer reviews.

1909 Los Angeles mayor Arthur Harper is forced to resign, due to his visits and ties to Los Angeles's red-light district.

1909 Prostitution is outlawed in Los Angeles.

ACKNOWLEDGMENTS

William Deverell, chair, Department of History, University of Southern California and Director, Huntington-USC Institute on California and the American West.

Jenny Wyatt and Erin Chase, the Huntington Library Photo Department.

Octavio Olvera and Simon Elliott, UCLA Special Collections.

John Cahoon, the Seaver Center.

The Central Library of the Los Angeles Public Library.

Bieneke Rare Book and Manuscript Library, Yale University.

Additional thanks to Sam Watters, Louise Bernard, Timothy Young, John Rechy, Jennifer Augustyn, Booth Moore, and Adam Tschorn at the *Los Angeles Times;* Bill Wolfsthal (Skyhorse Publishing/Sears Catalogue); Randall Young, Lauren Redness, Alia Penner, and to P.E.G., and T.G.

Gratitude to Bryan Gomez for his dedication, and to Dan Johnson and Leslie Chang.

Illustrations by Costanza Theodoli-Braschi.

Art direction by Will Staehle, with additional layout by Nancy Singer.

Special thanks to Judith Regan and her team at Regan Arts, including Lucas Wittman, Richard Ljoenes, and Kurt Andrews.

EPHEMERA &
PHOTOGRAPHY
CREDITS

———————•———————

Courtesy of The Huntington Library, San Marino, CA, viii-iv, xiv, 2-3, 6-7, 16, 22, 34, 65, 76, 83, 84, 85, 98, 104, 119, 120-121, 140-141, 150, 164-165, 169, 179, 217; Seaver Center for Western History Research, Los Angeles County Museum of Natural History, x, xi, xii, xiii, 14-15, 32-33, 35, 96-97, 124, 132-133, 156, 158-159, 182-183, 192-193, 218-219, 221; p. 95, Henry H. West (123), Photographers' Collection (Collection 98), UCLA Library Special Collections, Charles E. Young Research Library, UCLA, 8; Author's Private Collection, 11, 71, 80-81; Neg #A 610 - Los Angeles - Views (Business Enterprises), UCLA Library Special Collections, Charles E. Young Research Library, UCLA, 17; Jay T. Last Collection, The Huntington Library, San Marino, CA, 19, 39, 41, 42-43, 45, 116, 198; #9975 LA Views - Adams St. to Main St. (99), UCLA Library Special Collections, Charles E. Young Research Library, UCLA, 23; #D864 LA Views - Adams St. to Main St. (99), UCLA Library Special Collections, Charles E. Young Research Library, UCLA, 28-29; #1703 Folder 13, Ana Bégué de Packman Papers (Collection 1491) - Broadway (1), UCLA Library Special Collections, Charles E. Young Research Library, UCLA, 30-31; p. 98, Henry H. West (123), Photographers' Collection (Collection 98), UCLA Library Special Collections, Charles E. Young Research Library, UCLA, 36; Courtesy of Library of Congress, LC-USZ62-101143, 79; p. 94, Henry H. West (123), UCLA Library Special Collections, Charles E. Young Research Library, UCLA, 88, 93; p. 93, Henry H. West (123), UCLA Library Special Collections, Charles E. Young Research Library, UCLA, 92; Los Angeles Athletic Club and allied clubs (Call Number GV563. L67 1933), UCLA Library Special Collections, Charles E. Young Research Library, UCLA, 102-103; Photograph by Edouart & Son, Los Angeles, from California Views of the R.W. Waterman Family Papers, 04291, The Bancroft Library, University of California, Berkeley, 126-127; Ronald G. Becker Collection of Charles Eisenmann Photographs, Special Collections Research Center, Syracuse University Libraries, 130; Courtesy of United States Patent and Trademark Office, 147; The Druggist's Ready Reference. Morisson, Plummer & Company, 1880, pp. 224. Minnesota Historical Society, 153; p. 101, Henry H. West (123), Photographers' Collection (Collection 98), UCLA Library Special Collections, Charles E. Young Research Library, UCLA, 154; Folder 16, Ana Bégué de Packman Papers (Collection 1491) - Chinatown (1), UCLA Library Special Collections, Charles E. Young Research Library, UCLA, 162-163; Folder 18, Ana Bégué de Packman Papers (Collection 1491) - Churches 1870-1923 (2), UCLA Library Special Collections, Charles E. Young Research Library, UCLA, 170-171; #2037, Folder 18, Ana Bégué de Packman Papers (Collection 1491) - Churches 1870-1923 (2), UCLA Library Special Collections, Charles E. Young Research Library, UCLA, 172-173; Courtesy of Los Angeles Times, 174, 189; #7499 Folder 16, Ana Bégué de Packman Papers (Collection 1491) - Chinatown (1), UCLA Library Special Collections, Charles E. Young Research Library, UCLA, 176-177; Courtesy of Library of Congress, LC-USZC4-1845, 205; Courtesy of Library of Congress, British Cartoon Prints Collection, LC-USZ62-59623, 213; #094/057 Forbes Album, UCLA Library Special Collections, Charles E. Young Research Library, UCLA, 222-223; Keegan Allen, 241.

Liz Goldwyn is an author, filmmaker, and artist. She is the writer and director of the documentary *Pretty Things* (HBO, 2005). She is author of the nonfiction book *Pretty Things: the Last Generation of American Burlesque Queens* (HarperCollins). Goldwyn's short films include *Underwater Ballet* (2008), *L.A. at Night* (2009), *The Painted Lady* (2012), and *Dear Diary* (2013). Goldwyn was New York editor of *French Vogue* from 2001 to 2002 and has contributed to publications including *The New York Times Magazine, The Financial Times, British Vogue,* and *C Magazine*. In September 2014 she became the first guest editor of *Town & Country* in its 168-year history. Goldwyn lives and works in her hometown of Los Angeles.

Regan Arts.

65 Bleecker Street
New York, NY 10012

This book is a work of fiction.

First Regan Arts edition, October 2015

Library of Congress Control Number: 2015938258

ISBN 978-1-941393-04-8

Interior design by Will Staehle and Nancy Singer
Cover design by Will Staehle

Printed in China

10 9 8 7 6 5 4 3 2 1